Brome County

Tales from the Townships Book 1

By

Stephen Gobby

To my children, Chris & Jen

Also by Stephen Gobby

Of Brothers and Assassins

The author respectfully acknowledges that, before the arrival of European settlers, the geographical area depicted in this story was inhabited by the Abenaki.

Table of Contents

Chapter 1
The Last Days of Cannabis Crime

2018

Finn Toomey was standing in the ditch, next to a fenced-in pasture located on Sugar Hill Road. He stood with one arm on the top of a fence post and he watched intently as two roans grazed peacefully on the lush grasses. He checked his phone: 9:05. Stubs was late. Again. He should have known better than to ask Stubs to come help mend the fence.

Finn turned and looked in both directions for any sign of his friend's flashy, red Camaro. Stubs liked to call it his chick magnet but Finn told him that it was more like a cop magnet as far as he was concerned. Stubs would be driving slowly as was his custom on dirt roads. He was paranoid about getting dings and scratches from flying stones and whatnot. But, no. Nothing. No sign of Stubs. He went back to the horses. The pair had moved closer together, now standing head-to-tail, each swishing the other's face with their tail. He wondered how they did that: communicate that it's time to stop grazing and to start shooing away flies. Amazing. He continued to study the two horses. It was a pastoral scene if he ever did see one and all the more so because the sun shone brightly, just off to the east with only a few non-threatening clouds in the sky. But Finn knew all too well that the weather, much like life, was subject to change without notice.

Finn heard a car and turned toward the sound, but it wasn't Stubs. Instead, two drab-colored sedans braked hard and skidded to a stop only yards away from Finn, in a cloud of dust and gravel that caused a kind of dirt tornado. Four undercover cops, two from each car, jumped out and rushed toward Finn, yelling and screaming in French.

"A genoux, mon tabernacle! Bouges pas, mon hostie!"

Finn knew exactly what they were saying but he played dumb because he was an Anglo in a Francophone land and figured that if he was going down, he was going down in English, goddamnit. He also had the urge to crack wise about the nonsensical aspect of their command, the paradox of it all, like *Do I get on my knees or do I freeze? Which is it?* But being a smart ass while you're getting arrested is not recommended. It can get you roughed up. So, Finn just raised his arms, palms up, as if to say, *Hey, what's going on? How can I help?*

There were four cops: three men and one woman. His eyes locked on her first—she was his age, no more than twenty-five or twenty-six. Then Finn watched in alarm as the biggest cop, a guy with a face like a baboon, came at him. He did not resist, but even so the guy body-slammed him to the ground. Finn's face was pressed into the dewy grass, and he felt another cop's knee press into his neck. Agent Baboon slapped handcuffs on him, wrists behind his back. The two other male cops helped Finn to turn over and sat him up on the ground. Then, each taking an underarm they dragged him so he sat with his back against a fence post.

The three males went off to search Finn's pickup truck. But not the female cop. Her job was to watch Finn. He wasn't sure if that was because she was a junior cop or that she was a boss or a supervisor. Finn forced himself not to watch where exactly the men were searching inside that truck. The female cop was cute though, thought Finn, wearing these tight jeans, a black tee shirt, and sexy ankle boots with a thick heel. Sweet, he thought. Of course, she also wore a badge on her belt and a 9mm on her right hip.

The three cops emerged from the truck, Agent Baboon with a dime bag in his hand, waving it in the air, grinning, like he had just won the lotto. They now approached Finn, and Agent Baboon did all the talking. Finn was still on the ground, looking up at that strange face of the angry cop. The long snout on him.

"C'est quoi ton nom, mon hostie?"

"Mon hostie?" asked Finn.

"C'est quoi ton nom?" Baboon repeated.

"Finn. My name is Finn."

"That's not a name. That's da part of that fish."

"Well, you sure landed a big one today, didn't you?" said Finn.

A puzzled look came over Agent Baboon's face. He shot a glance at the cute lady cop but she just shook her head, dismissing Finn's comments as irrelevant.

Agent Baboon and the lady cop helped Finn to his feet but it was she who ushered Finn to their car. She was tall, only two or three inches shorter than Finn's six feet. She had her left hand at his right elbow as they walked and as strange as it was under the circumstance, he enjoyed the feel of her hand on him. She opened the back door for him, he got in and she closed the door. She and Agent Baboon got in and Baboon put it in drive. They began their trek to Cowansville, or at least that was where Finn hoped they were heading. If these cops were from headquarters in Sherbrooke or Montreal, Finn would be going on a little road trip. Finn's fingers were crossed for the much closer Cowansville.

Finn turned in his seat and looked out the rear window. He saw the two remaining cops standing next to his pickup, talking. He was hoping they wouldn't strip it down, tear it apart, like they did in the movies. Finn turned back in his seat. Out the front windshield of the police car he saw a pickup approaching, and as it got closer, he recognized the truck and the driver. It was Truman Lightfoot. The owner of the horses and the pasture; the fellow who had hired him to repair the fence. As Truman passed, he looked into the car and it was clear he had recognized Finn. Awkward.

Finn settled back into his seat and prepared for the trip to . . . wherever. But it was hard to get comfortable with his hands cuffed behind his back. He wondered if he would be able to slip his hands down below his ass, down to his ankles and then back up onto his lap. That would be a good trick and he figured he was nimble enough to pull it off. But the cops in front would probably not appreciate his agility. For sure he'd find his face pressed into the parking lot surface when they got there. Agent Baboon would probably rough him up again. But not the lady cop. She looked nice. He couldn't picture her roughing anyone up. God, she was cute.

Finn was still trying to figure out where they were going when the odor struck him. The back seat was beginning to release pungent aromas of old burgers, donuts and funky poutine gravy. Gross, he thought. He presumed it was Agent Baboon's car. He seriously doubted the lady cop would have a car that smelled foul.

When they came to Stagecoach Road they turned right toward Brome Village. They drove right past Finn's house in the village, and he turned to watch his front door disappear into the distance. They passed the Brome fairgrounds and turned right onto the 215. At Owen's Corner, they turned left, west onto the 104. Phew, he thought. That meant they were heading to Cowansville and he could maybe get these cuffs off soon.

At the station they removed the cuffs and processed Finn, taking his fingerprints and photos. Then it was off to the interrogation room where he sat for a while, alone, cooling his heels. He wasn't worried. That was a tactic the cops used to get someone to feel dejected and alone, almost looking forward to a friendly face entering the room, to break the monotony, to start a conversation, and the desired effect of it all was to extract a confession.

The door opened and Agent Baboon and the cute cop entered the room and sat themselves across from Finn. They slid their business cards across the table towards him. He looked at hers first. Jojo Alison. Ah, he thought. A compatriot. An Anglo. An ally. Sweet. He was going to be okay. He then read her partner's card. François

Babouin. Holy shit! Babouin is French for baboon. No way! Going through life with that name, and that face? No wonder this guy was in a foul mood, throwing innocent people to the ground, roughing them up for no reason.

Agent Babouin asked again for Finn's name.

"Finnian Toomey," he said, "but my friends call me Finn. You can call me Finn. You are my friends, right?"

Babouin asked him where he lived.

"Brome Village."

He asked Finn what he had to say for himself and then dropped the dime bag of dope on the table.

"I don't know anything about that," said Finn. "You guys planted that in my truck. I don't deal in narcotics. I am a law-abiding citizen."

"Today," Agent Babouin insisted, poking his finger on the table, "you will make a declaration."

"Okay," said Finn, "I declare I'll have a beer, s'il vous plait. Toute de fuckin' suite." Now Finn was poking his finger on the table. Finn thought he detected Agent Alison suppressing a smile.

Agent Babouin was fuming and looked like he was about to jump at him over the table, but Agent Jojo tapped him on the shoulder. Finn got the impression that Agent Babouin was jaded. Too many years on the job maybe. He was definitely the older cop there, maybe mid-fifties. But Agent Jojo was another matter. She was young and pleasant. And quite the looker. She was tall and athletic looking. Not a flaw about her. She wore her dirty blond hair back in a ponytail. Actually, Finn thought she might have had a thing for him. But Finn wasn't born yesterday. He knew they were a team, cute cop, bad cop, united in their singular purpose of getting him to confess and then march him off to a holding cell. So, Finn put romance out of his mind. For the moment.

Agent Babouin continued. "Where you get the marijuana?"

"From you," said Finn.

"No, we take it from you, in your truck, under that back seat."

"Oh, no! You planted it there!"

Again, Agent Jojo touched Babouin on the shoulder and quietly suggested that he go get a coffee. She motioned with her head for him to leave the room.

Agent Babouin rose, scowled at Finn, and left the room. Agent Jojo closed the file folder on the table, rolled her chair around and away from behind the table so there was nothing between her and Finn. Ever so slightly, she leaned in, closing the distance between them, but not too close, and looked Finn in the eye.

"Finn," she said, "we all make mistakes. You made a mistake. It's alright. Not a big deal. We can work this out. We can make it right."

Finn smiled. "Okay. But may I ask you a question?"

"Sure," she said.

"Are you feeling this?" Finn gestured with his hands. "You and me? This chemistry? Are you aroused right now?"

"Wow, Finn. What the hell?" said Jojo. She stood up quickly, the back of her knees sending her chair rolling back so it hit the wall. She looked down at him.

"Well, this is a conversation gone bad, isn't it? Now I could respond by saying, yeah, I get excited when I bust scumbags like you, but I won't say that. Instead, I'll take the high road."

She reached over for her chair, brought it back and after a moment of thought, she sat down again. "I'll be the adult in the room," she said, "and try and de-escalate, so I'll ask you, why would you say that, Finn? What did you hope to gain? I mean, did I disrespect you somehow? I don't think I did. If you don't want to talk to me, you don't have to. Just say so. You can talk to my partner," she said pointing with her thumb to the door. "But don't insult me. There's no need for that. It's not going to get you anywhere."

Finn thought he saw one of her blue eyes become moist, just a little. He became aware that he might actually have upset her. This was the strangest police interrogation that Finn had ever experienced. Aside from speeding tickets and the like, he had only been questioned by police twice before but this was his first with a female cop. He had figured he could take charge of the conversation by making her uncomfortable with the comment about being aroused. But, she had regained control immediately, chastising him like he was a teenage boy. He wondered if that talent was typical of female cops or was Agent Jojo special.

"You know what?" said Finn. "You're right. I'm sorry. That was rude. And uncalled for. I apologize."

"Good," she said. "Apology accepted. Now we're making progress."

Finn nodded.

"Now let me ask *you* a question, Finn."

"Sure."

"We read you your rights. Offered you a lawyer but you didn't call one. Why not?"

"I don't need a lawyer," he said. "Anything happens, I can handle it. Even in court. I'm not worried."

"Fair enough," she said.

Finn was curious about something but wasn't sure she would answer him. He took a chance. "Can I ask you another question?"

"Sure," she said, lifting her index finger. "But keep it polite."

"I promise," he said. "Were you disappointed with what you found?"

"You mean in your truck?"

"Yeah."

"Yes, we were disappointed, actually," she admitted.

"You expected more?"

"Yes," she said. "The mother lode, in fact."

"You do know where you got your information from, right?"

"I can't comment on that, Finn," she said. "You know that. Why don't you tell me who you think it was."

"No way," said Finn. "I'm no name-dropper." As he said it, Finn knew that he had misused the term *name-dropper*. He had no idea why he had done that. "But I will say this," continued Finn, "the person who gave you this information is the one with *the mother lode.*

"Is that right?" she said.

"Yes, of course. He's the only one who knew that I had a dime bag and where I kept it because he sold it to me. Officer, you've been duped."

"So, you're admitting that you had it in your truck and that we didn't plant it?"

"Of course, I admit it. I'm not worried. Grass will be legal any day now. Worst case scenario, the judge will bang his gavel, give me a small fine and say bye-bye. That is, if your crown prosecutor even decides to proceed. I doubt that he will. We are in the last days of cannabis crime. You know that, right? We all know it.

"Agent Alison just nodded. "You may be right about small quantities, Finn, but not about mother lodes. Those quantities will always remain illegal. And until I am no longer required by law to consider dime bags illegal, I will consider them illegal. I will do my job."

10

That was a revelation to Finn. He had thought that all cannabis would be decriminalized. His information was wrong. He'd best not let it show that this was news to him. "I hear you," said Finn, "but I gotta say it hurts for me to think of all this fine product going down the drain. Or up in smoke. However you guys dispose of it. Or do you guys like, *confiscate* it if you get my drift?" Finn brought his fingers to his lips as though taking a toke.

Jojo smiled and said, "Finn, I can tell you this much; my job is worth much more than a cheap high. Plus I have my hands full with cheap bourbon and beer, if you get *my* drift." She smiled devilishly.

"Yes, I do," he said, smiling. Oh, she was a charmer, thought Finn.

"I have another question," said Finn. He hoped he wasn't pushing his luck on asking questions but he figured, why not.

"Shoot."

"Well, you and Agent Babouin work here at the detachment?"

"Yes," she said.

"I thought drugs were handled by special squads in Montreal and Sherbrooke."

"So, you're wondering why we got involved."

"Yes," said Finn. "Not that it's any of my business."

"The guys from HQ are really busy and won't come out unless it's for a sure thing. And something big."

"Ah," Finn said.

"If we had found the *mother lode*, they would have come out to take over the case.

"Okay," said Finn. "I get it."

There was a knock on the door. Agent Jojo got up and opened it. In came her partner, Agent Babouin, who handed her Finn's truck keys. She looked at the keys and slid them across the table towards Finn.

"We have all your info," she said. "We'll contact you if we move forward with charges."

"Okay," said Finn, rising from his chair. "Fair enough. And my truck?"

"It's just out back," she said. "Come. I'll take you to it."

All three exited the interrogation room. Agent Babouin turned to the left and Agent Alison said, "This way," as she headed to the right.

Finn followed her down a hallway while he fiddled nervously with his keys in his right hand. A uniformed cop came through the door at the end of the hallway, the door to which they were heading, he nodded to Agent Jojo as he passed. He also gave Finn a once-over. As that door slowly closed, Finn caught a glimpse of at least two police cars. They were headed to the garage. He hoped that his truck wasn't there, hoisted up on a lift, all dismantled, like they had done in *The French Connection:* disheveled cops sitting around, drinking coffee out of paper cups, scratching their heads, frustrated after having taken the vehicle apart, piece by piece, and *not* having found the narcotics they were led to believe were hidden inside.

Finn followed Jojo into the garage. He looked around. His truck was not there.

"It's out back," said Jojo as though she knew what he was thinking. And perhaps she did.

Finn followed her through the door leading outside. As they rounded the corner of the station, he saw his truck. It was in the parking lot at the rear of the station. It was intact, parked neatly in its space. It looked fine.

As they approached the truck, Jojo turned and said, "One of the other officers drove it here so there's no towing fee."

"Cool," said Finn but silently he thought, why would he pay a towing fee if he wasn't being charged with anything? But he let it go. Sometimes, when they tell you that you have the right to remain silent, it's best to do just that.

Agent Alison stood there while he unlocked his truck and opened the door.

"You take care, Finn," she said.

"I will. And you too."

She nodded and turned to walk away. Finn was about to step up into his truck when he stopped.

"Agent Alison?" he said.

She stopped and turned around. "Yes?"

"I'm sorry about the way I talked to you earlier. There was no call for that."

She smiled softly. "That's okay, Finn. No harm done. But please try and stay out of trouble."

"Yeah," he said unconvincingly. "Hey, so, maybe I could give you a call sometime. You know, we could hang out? Maybe grab a beer?"

"Yeah, Finn," she said, "don't do that. François is like a father to me. He'd come after you, something fierce."

"Only if someone told him about it." Finn smirked.

She smiled a smile that totally disarmed him. He didn't know what to say. He stepped up into his truck, shut the door, and waved. He waved like an idiot, like a high school kid might wave to a female teacher he'd seen unexpectedly at the shopping centre.

She wiggled her fingers, turned and walked back toward the garage door.

Finn shook his head to clear his mind. He started up his truck and drove off. As he left the detachment parking lot, he mocked himself. *Sorry about the way I talked to you earlier. Jesus.*

Finn drove north up the 202 until he reached the 104 where he stopped for a red light. He turned right and headed east, towards Brome County and Brome Village, his home and native land. He decided to stop at the service station at Gilman's Corner to fill up with gas. When he finished pumping, he looked around to make sure he was alone and went to the rear of the truck. He got on one knee and reached under the bed of the truck, then worked his fingers up to the top side of the spare tire. It was still there. Snuggly and securely duct-taped to the wheel part of the spare tire: a package about the size of a kilo of sugar. Sweet.

As Finn drove home along Stagecoach Road, two names were whirling about in his brain. One was Jojo Alison, foxy lady cop. The second was Stubs. *Stubs, you back-stabbing son of a bitch.* Stubs was the only person Finn had told that he kept his stash taped under the back seat of his pickup truck. Of course, Finn hadn't gone on to tell him that that was his decoy stash; that his real stash was taped to his spare tire. Also, how did the cops know where Finn would be at 9 a.m.? Stubs. And who didn't show up at his rendezvous, at the precise time the cops were about to arrest Finn? Stubs.

So, yeah, thought Finn. *You sold me out, Stubs. Big time. And now you're gonna pay. Big time.*

Chapter 2
Autumn Leaves

2023

Jojo Alison punched her pin onto the keypad of the lock on her front door, opened it and stepped aside to let Andrew in. They hung their coats in the hallway, removed their shoes and made their way to the kitchen. Jojo went to the island and began gathering what she needed to make an apple crisp while Andrew walked to the window that looked out over the backyard and a small forest beyond. He stood there motionless, just gazing into the trees.

"Hey, babe, I'm going to get started on that apple crisp I promised you," she said.

"Okay," he said, still at the window.

"Do you want anything to drink?"

"No thanks," he said.

Andrew was quiet today. They were just getting back from a long walk and he hadn't been at all talkative during that time. She had tried to make conversation but anything she said was met with either a grunt or a shrug or a verbal *I dunno*. But this was not her first rodeo. She knew very well that when your boyfriend goes silent, it speaks volumes. And if police work had taught her anything over the years, it was patience. How to be patient with people. Always be patient was the cop's golden rule. Until the time for patience had passed and it was time to take care of business. So he'd better snap out of it soon because her patience was wearing thin. Soon she would call him on it. Life was too short for passive aggressive silliness. Whatever it was, they could talk about it but for that to happen, he had to actually talk.

"What's happening out there," Jojo asked. "What's that noise?"

"Your neighbor with his leaf blower."

Jojo was slicing her third apple, thinking about how untidy her own lawn was beginning to look and how much she really didn't care. "Now there's a dumb invention for you," she said. "The leaf blower. Never understood the need for that thing. Leaves are good for the soil. My leaves stay right there on the ground."

"I have a leaf blower," Andrew said.

"Get out of here," she said smiling. "You do not."

"Actually, I do. I have a leaf blower. I keep it in my garage. With all my gardening tools."

"Shit, I didn't know that," she said, embarrassed yet almost snickering. "Sorry."

Jojo picked up the cutting board and slid the sliced apples into the aluminum mixing bowl. She went back to slicing.

"Alexa," said Jojo, "play some Van Morrison please."

Alexa responded: *Playing music by Van Morrison* and *Into the Mystic* began playing on her smart speaker.

Jojo was still slicing apples when Andrew turned and slowly approached the kitchen island.

"Could you turn off the music?"

"Sure," she said. "Alexa, stop the music, please."

Andrew put his hands on the back of a barstool and looked directly at her.

Jojo looked back at him, her hand hovering over the bowl. He had a strange look on his face. Something she had not seen before. It had a child-like vulnerability to it—a child trying to behave like an adult. This was obviously not something that was easy for him. She braced for the worst.

"Jojo, there is something I have to talk to you about."

"Shoot," she said. "I'm all ears."

"I don't know how to say it."

"Just say it," she urged.

"Jojo, it's over."

"What's over?"

"We're over," he said. "I don't want to do this anymore. I'm very sorry."

Jojo looked away and put down the knife. She took a dish cloth and wiped her hands.

"Okay," she said. "It's . . . it's not about the leaf blower comment, is it?"

"No."

She hesitated. "It's about the shooting . . . the shooting in Sutton."

"Yes," he said. "I—my family and I—we still can't get past this."

"I understand," she said. "I get it."

"Well, we don't get it," he said. "I mean, it's insane. Everyone gets off scot-free. No one is held accountable."

"Well," she said, "Claude Laforce was exonerated by the coroner and by the *Bureau des enquêtes indépendantes*. But I understand. It was a terrible tragedy. It's okay. Whatever, Andrew. Whatever."

"Laforce was exonerated," Andrew said, "because he acted according to police policy and procedure. You see a gun, you shoot. Even though Tommy Whitecraft was only sixteen years old, and it wasn't a real gun."

Jojo took a breath. "No. Laforce was exonerated because a police officer is justified in shooting when they feel their life is in danger. And it looked like a real gun. I thought it was. Everyone there did. It was a replica, and he was 6 foot 2. We didn't know he was a kid."

"A kid versus four cops. You included. And no one gets punished or suspended or even reprimanded."

"We went through the process, Andrew. And you know that. Laforce was just exonerated. It's not like they gave him a medal."

"But they gave you a promotion, didn't they."

"What? What the fuck did you just say?"

"Yeah, you just got your corporal stripes."

"You asshole!" she said. That hit hard, that he really thought she had been handed the promotion instead of having earned it. She felt tears welling up inside but she suppressed them. *Stay mad. Don't Cry.* "I passed my exams two years ago and I was waiting for a posting when one became available here in Cowansville. They offered it to me so I took it. It had nothing to do with the shooting. Jesus Christ, Andrew."

"Still," he said.

"No one was happy about the shooting," she said. "We were all devastated. Do you think we wanted to kill a teenager? Or anyone for that matter? We are not a bunch of trigger-happy mercenaries."

"Why didn't Laforce aim for his legs?"

"Andrew, we've been over this more than once. I don't know why you can't hear me. We are not snipers. We are not trained to aim for the legs. Legs are a small target. If you aim for the legs you can miss and hit someone else. And bullets can ricochet off the asphalt. Plus, a shooter wounded in the legs can still fire and hurt or kill people. We aim for body mass. That's how we are trained."

"Well then change your training."

"Look," she said, trying to calm down, "the coroner recommended that there be more training for police on how to better deal with people in crisis. I think that's going to happen."

Jojo picked up the dishcloth and then dropped it in frustration. She shook her head.

"It's nice, isn't it," she said, "to have hours, days and weeks, even months, to discuss and analyze and judge a decision that a police officer has to make in a fraction of a second, in the heat of action."

Andrew's eyes drifted to the bowl of sliced apples. He then turned his head, looking back at the window where he had been standing earlier. Not only was he not going to concede to her, now he wouldn't even look at her. She understood non-verbal communication. He wanted out of here. He wanted to be gone. He was done.

"Okay," said Jojo. "Enough. I understand your point of view and I accept it. Let's not get into it all over again for no reason. And I understand that you can't get past this. So, it's okay. It's over, I understand. Please let's not fight about it. You deserve to be happy and to be with someone you respect. So, let's just leave it there."

"Well, thank you for your understanding." He hesitated then said, "Will you be okay?"

"Will I be okay?" she said. "Of course, I'll be okay. What am I, thirteen years old?"

"Oh . . . good."

"Actually," said JoJo, "I am a little relieved to tell you the truth."

"You are?"

She could see that he was taken aback. "Yes. We've been going out, like three months now and I was thinking that we are not really that compatible. You're a nice guy and very kind but I don't think we are meant for each other. I've been questioning our relationship over the past while too, wondering whether this should go on, whether we should continue."

"I don't understand," said Andrew. "What do you mean, not compatible?"

"I really don't want to get into it," said Jojo, "because we're breaking up so what's the point? But I think this is all for the best. Come," she said, leading Andrew by the arm–almost as she would a suspect–and gently walking him to the front door. "I wish only the best for you. You are a great guy."

She grabbed his coat from the coat rack and held it while he turned and slipped his arms into the sleeves. She leaned over and placed his shoes in front of him. He tried slipping them on without bending but it wasn't working. His shoes wouldn't cooperate. They kept slipping and flipping around. He finally bent down and used a finger.

"It's better this way," she said, opening the door.

Andrew stood there for a moment, as though he was about to say something, but Jojo slowly began closing the door, almost pushing him out.

"Take good care," she said as she latched the door shut.

Through the peephole, she could see he was still standing there.

She walked back to the kitchen and began putting things away. She returned the unpeeled apples to the fridge, along with the mixing bowl, half full of sliced apples. Then she moved toward the window and looked out at the empty trees.

So, it was the promotion that did it. Well, the shooting didn't help but her promotion probably hammered the final nail into the coffin. It was coming back to her now. Three weeks earlier she had invited him to the Rendez-Vous Café in Cowansville, their favorite spot, to break the exciting news to him. Her promotion had come through and she was staying in Cowansville. She was doubly excited by that fact because a promotion, more often than not, meant a transfer to some distant detachment like Abitibi or the Gaspé. But she was staying here, in Cowansville. Now, she remembered the look on his face. He was nonplussed. Definitely not a look of jubilation she might have expected. And there was no *Hurray, congratulations, Babe, and you're staying here and we can continue our relationship.* Instead a fake, forced smile crinkled his lips and his eyes were empty. She was so excited that day, that she barely took notice of his mood. But it was coming back to her now. It was the same kind of reaction that his family had exhibited when he had first brought her to a family BBQ. Fake smiles all around and only one person spoke to her; Andrew's brother Randy and all he did was complain about all the times he and his buddies had been stopped by the SQ and hassled for no reason. He actually asked her how she felt about being the token Anglophone in a completely French-speaking police force. Again, thinking about it now, that moment at the Rendez-Vous Café, when she told him about her promotion, was probably the moment he decided to end the relationship. But it took him three weeks to muster the courage to do the deed. Whatever, she thought.

She grabbed her phone to make sure the gym was still open. It was Sunday after all. Yes, open till five. She went to her bedroom to get her gym bag. She pushed her clothing around in the gym bag to make sure her padded gloves were there. She felt like pounding the heavy bag today.

She took her bag to the living room and checked through the window to make sure Andrew's pickup was gone. It was. She went to the garage, got into her car, and drove to the gym.

Ninety minutes later, Jojo emerged from the gym on Rue Sud in Cowansville, got into her car and drove north. She turned right on Rue Principale and headed east. She came to a stop at James and then at Desourdy. She smiled when she passed the house on Main street that she had rented previously, until she bought her house. She continued then slowed down at the courthouse and came to a full stop at the stop sign at the Brome-Mississquoi-Perkins hospital. She continued a few hundred meters and turned left onto Rue Peron and climbed the hill to Les Hauteurs de Sweetsburg or Sweetsburg Heights, as her father liked to call it. She turned onto rue Sweetsburg and she smiled a little again upon seeing her house. She turned left again into her driveway and then into the garage.

She was extremely happy with her purchase, this new home, almost two years ago. She recalled when her colleague, François Babouin had told her about this new subdivision.

"C'est de toute beauté," he had said. "Tu vas adorer ça. Je te le garantie."

Indeed, it was love at first sight. It was clad in natural wood with black trimmings, and it sat high, above the town of Cowansville. She loved the house and so did her parents. It had been a little out of her price range, but Mom and Dad offering to help their only child with the down payment, made it all possible.

And the view . . . off to the left or south side, she had a stunning vista of Lac-Davignon. And from the southeast corner of the house, from either the panoramic window in her bedroom or from out on the deck, she had an unobstructed view of the mountains of Brome County. She could see the ski hills of Mount Sutton and, on a clear day, Jay Peak in Vermont.

At the rear of the house, off to the right, there stood a pretty little forested area. Every once in a while, she saw a family of deer wander through it. She had no delusions, though. Even though the salespeople had denied it, she was pretty certain that the forest would be dozed some day to make room for more homes. Nothing lasts forever, she thought. But for now, while it was there, she would enjoy it.

She walked to her bedroom and realized she was still perspiring from her workout. She didn't like to shower at the gym. She saved that for home. So, she undressed and threw her clothing into the laundry basket. She then picked up the laundry basket and brought it to the bathroom and placed it on the washer. She got into the shower. When she was done, she dried off, wrapped the towel around herself then looked at her hair in the mirror. She tousled her hair with her fingers and thought that was good enough. She wasn't going anywhere today. She went back to her bedroom and put on a warm cotton sweat suit and warm socks. She returned to the bathroom and put the towel and the contents of her laundry basket into the washer.

Something caught her eye. She reached down into the washer and pulled out a large black T-shirt. She held it up in front of her. *Pink Floyd – Another Brick in the Wall*. She reached for a trash bag on the shelf above the washer and dryer and threw the T-shirt into the bag and tied a knot in it. She turned and went to the garage and placed it into the large trash bin. She returned to the bathroom, added a soap pod to the clothing, closed the lid of the washer and pushed *START.*

In the kitchen she washed everything she had used to prepare the apple crisp. She opened the fridge and took out the mixing bowl of sliced apples. She looked at them for a moment then slowly scooped them into the compost container on the counter. She washed the bowl and put it away. Her phone beeped. She picked it up. It was a text message from Andrew. Of course, it was. She deleted the text without reading it then blocked the number. *No goddamn way*, she thought. They were not doing that.

She walked to the window overlooking the backyard and the small forest beyond, where Andrew had been standing earlier that day, gathering his courage to break up with her. It was a cloudy, dreary day, and the trees, which until two weeks ago had been in glorious color, were now mostly bare. The fall foliage had been spectacular this year. And it had lasted longer than usual, it seemed. It was strange how some years the colors seemed more stunning, more vivid than in other years and she wondered why. She wondered if there was some scientific explanation for it. But that was all over. The trees would go dormant now. Not dead. Just dormant. And they would stay dormant and awaken only after the vernal equinox, at the change of seasons, in spring, when the warmth of nature would bring them back to life, to produce buds and then leaves once again. She looked forward to that. But for now, like the man said, "it was over".

She went to the living room, sat down on the sofa, turned on the TV and spent forty minutes going through possible titles on Netflix. Nothing grabbed her. She turned off the TV and tried reading. She was working on her mom's latest novel: *Runaway* by Joanna Alison. But after a few pages she returned the page marker to where it had been: at the beginning of chapter 3. She didn't like this. She was having trouble concentrating. She got up and went to her bedroom. She grabbed a pillow from under the covers and lay down. She had a smart speaker in her bedroom, so she asked Alexa to play "Into the Mystic" by Van Morrison.

Jojo curled up tight on her side with the pillow against her tummy and she slowly drifted off, into that other world, somewhere between slumber and consciousness, into the mystic, where she soared like an eagle above lush, green mountain tops and then sailed amid gentle, blue ocean waves, all the while sensing the essence of bitterness, sadness, resentment, and disappointment.

Jojo woke up at five pm to the sound of a text coming in on her phone. She looked. It was Dad.

Free to talk? He wrote.

Yes! She responded. She put the pillow behind her back and sat up in bed.

The phone rang and she answered, "Hi."

"Hey, Jojo. How are you?"

"I'm good, Dad. You?"

"Just fine. I did some house cleaning today and I just got in from tidying up outside a bit. I got the flower garden ready for winter. I pruned all the perennials. That took a while. I put the patio furniture away too. Bunch of stuff like that. Gotta be ready when the snows come. You know how it is: there's always something to do."

"Oh, I know. Hey, do you ever use a leaf blower?"

"What? No. I don't have one of those. I don't believe in them. That's a dumb machine, moving a mess from one place to another. Why do you ask? Did you buy one?"

"No, I don't have one and I feel the same way. I say leave leaves alone."

"Good for you, Jojo. But if you got a leaf blower, that's ok. You know that, right?"

"Yes, I know but I don't want one. I feel the same way you do. They are a silly machine. Hey, how's Mom?"

"She's just finishing up that book tour. She'll be home tomorrow. I pick her up at four in Dorval."

"Don't you miss Mom when she's traveling?"

"Oh, I miss her very much. Why do you ask?"

"Well, because didn't you used to travel with Mom? On her tours? You don't anymore."

"Yes, I did. The tours were fun. But your mom always pointed me out in the audience and she would introduce me. Then people would often ask questions about me and how much Mom's stories were based on my experiences in the Mounties. I felt I was stealing her thunder. Know what I mean?"

Jojo said she did.

"So at one point," he continued, "I said I would just stay home. And look after you."

"How come Mom never used her own name on her books?"

"Well," he said, "In the beginning, when she was starting out, she wasn't as confident about her writing as she is today and she felt that her name might be a hindrance in a literary career. Like your mom says, her name has eleven consonants with only 2 vowels and is pronounceable only by the people who come from the same Ukrainian village as her parents."

"Too funny."

"Yeah, she says her name it looks like a word puzzle, an anagram, something to decipher, more than someone's name. So, she decided to take Alison as her *nom de plume.*"

"Okay," said Jojo. "I get it. But did you ever tell Mom why you stopped going on her tours?"

"No. I don't think we ever talked about it."

"Maybe you should, Dad. So she knows that it's not because you didn't want to be there with her."

"Yeah, you're right," he said. "I should talk to her. I will."

"Okay, good," said Jojo. "And I'll text her hello later, before bedtime."

"Good," he said, "that's the best time to get her. When do you go back to work?"

"I go on at three, tomorrow afternoon."

"Ah, evening shift. The worst, right?"

"I don't mind it, actually. There's usually plenty of action and I have a good team so it's all good."

"Good," he said.

"Midnight to eight shifts are the worst for me," she said. "Wreaks havoc with my circadian rhythms."

"Ha," he said. "I hate when that happens."

"I have trouble sleeping in the daytime," she added.

"I totally understand. Actually, I used to enjoy the midnight to eight shift. Slept like a baby during the day. But that's me. Plus your mom kept the house very quiet for me."

"Mom is the best," said Jojo.

"Oh, you got that right," he said. "And so, what else is new? What's happening?"

"Well," she said, hesitating. "Andrew and I broke up."

"Andrew Lessard, right?"

"Yeah."

"Sorry about that. You broke off with him? What did he do?"

Jojo suddenly heard an immense thud coming from the rear deck. "Holy crap, Dad. Hang on!" Phone in hand, she got off the bed, ran out of the bedroom to the living room and to the patio door leading to the back deck. There on the floor of the deck, was a black bird.

"What the hell is going on, Jojo?"

"Sorry, Dad. A bird flew into the window off the rear deck. I think he's dead. No, wait. It's moving. Wait. It just stood up, Dad."

"What's he doing?"

"Just standing there."

"What kind of bird is it?"

"It's black. I think it's a fledgling crow. It's a sizable bird."

"What's he doing now?"

"He's just standing there, no, hold on." Jojo chuckled. "He just shook his head. Like he's saying, 'What happened?' Now he'd sort of just walking around. Hold on. He just flapped his wings. I think he might be getting ready to . . . okay, there he goes. He just flew off, Dad. He's gone. He's okay."

"Oh, good," he said.

Jojo started walking back to her bedroom but stopped instead and sat down on the living room sofa. "Funny thing, Dad."

"What's that?"

That bird just encapsulated our lives: fly around and enjoy life. If by chance you crash into some unseen or unforeseen obstacle, get back up, shake it off and start living your life again."

"So true," he said, laughing. "Now, where were we? Oh yeah, you were going to tell me why you broke off with Andrew."

"No, Dad. He broke off with me."

"Wow, that's unusual. You're usually the one doing the breaking up.

"Yes, I know but this time it was him." She hesitated. "Actually, when I heard that thud on the deck I thought maybe it was Andrew. Maybe returning something of mine that I had left at his place."

"Did you have a lot there? At his place?"

"No. Just a toothbrush."

"A toothbrush wouldn't have made that noise," he said.

"If it was wrapped with a brick it would."

He laughed. "Well, we know it wasn't a brick," he said. "So, tell me, how are you feeling?"

"I'm okay. But I have to say I thought about you when it was happening this afternoon. About what you told me way back when?"

"Really?"

"Yes. It was the best advice ever. You said, 'If someone is breaking up with you, make sure you keep your dignity. Don't let them see you cry. Don't give them the power. Don't beg, bargain or negotiate. It demeans you.' You remember telling me that?"

"Yes, I do. Good for you for remembering. Did you cry?"

"Hell no. We never cry in front of people who are hurting us. We cry later, with people who love us."

"Good girl," he said and she was pleased to hear the pride in his voice. "Did he give a reason?"

"It was about the shooting in Sutton. His family is close to Tommy Whitecraft's family. Totally understandable, I guess."

"Damn."

"But then I turned the tables on him. Like you taught me."

"You did? Good for you. Tell me, tell me."

"Yeah, I told him I was a little relieved that he was breaking up with me because I didn't think we were all that compatible. That I had been questioning our relationship, too, lately."

"Good one, Jojo. How'd he react?"

"Well, he wanted details but I told him we were breaking up and I didn't want to talk about it. What was the point now? Then I walked him to the door."

"Go girl! Have you heard from him?"

"He texted a little later, but I deleted it and blocked his number."

"That's my girl. Listen, Jojo, I know you're okay but do you want me to come over?"

"No, no, Dad. I'm fine."

"Okay, but don't be shy. I could bring a box of tissue. Like when you were young. Foster to Cowansville is like only twenty minutes."

"No, I'm okay. But thanks." She noticed she was fiddling with the drawstrings on the waist of her track pants. She shook her hands to stop. "Dad?"

"Yes?"

"He intimated that I got my promotion because of the shooting."

"Oh, that's messed up. That's not right. He doesn't understand how it works. What's he, a plumber, something like that?"

She smiled. "He's an electrician. Good and successful one too. He has four employees. He's a decent guy. And handsome. The shooting messed everything up. The Sutton community all banded together over it, like communities often do. Naturally, it turned almost everyone against the SQ within days."

"Yeah . . ."

"We're not killers, Dad. Shit, we don't go out wanting to shoot anyone, let alone a teenage boy."

"I know, Jojo. I know. It's a tough part of the job. In my thirty years as a Mountie I never had to shoot anyone and I am happy for that. But in truth, Jojo, neither did you. You didn't shoot anyone."

"I know, Dad. I know. But I was there. I was part of it. I was there. We were all there. I can't explain it."

"Yes, I understand," he said. He hesitated for a moment then continued, "Just changing topics for a moment, Jojo, maybe next time try dating a cop. They understand what it's like to be police."

"I can't do that, Dad. Men—especially men cops—are awful gossips. In no time I'd be the butt of jokes and conjecture, all kinds of shit. No thanks. If you're a female cop, you've got to keep your private life private. If you want to stay sane, that is."

"I understand. Well, I won't offer you any stupid platitudes at this point. Except maybe, 'this too shall pass'."

"Yes," said Jojo. "And 'keep passing the open windows'."

"Exactly," he said. "From John Irving's *The Hotel New Hampshire*. You remember that?"

"Of course. That goes back a bit but I do remember. Those were your words of encouragement after my break-up with my first boyfriend. I was heartbroken. What was I? Thirteen?"

"I remember that. But I think you were a little older than thirteen. What was his name again?"

"We don't know and we don't care, Dad. It's in the past."

"That's my girl."

"Of course, it's the opposite for birds. For them, it should: keep passing the closed windows."

"Good one, Jojo!"

"To be honest, Dad, I'm still not certain what those words mean."

"You mean, 'Keep passing the open windows'?" he asked.

"Yeah."

"Well, I think it can mean to keep passing windows of opportunity, maybe? As in don't date too soon? Or don't stare out the open windows, as in don't dwell on this too much. Think of other things instead."

"Or maybe it means, don't despair," she said, "as in don't jump out the open windows."

"Yes," he said, "there's that too. I think you may be right."

Of course she was right. She'd been traumatized by the shooting more than anyone could or would ever know. She hadn't fired that fatal shot but she was aiming at Tommy. All three of them were aiming. But Laforce was a certified sharpshooter. He took part in competitions. When the corporal on duty told Laforce to take the shot, she was relieved. But had she been ordered to, she knew she would have obeyed.

"Okay, Dad. I gotta go. I have things to do to get ready for tomorrow."

"Okay."

"Thanks for the call and the pep talk. I'll talk with Mom later."

"Perfect. Take care, Jojo. I love you."

"Love you too, Dad."

Jojo went to bed at ten-thirty that evening. She put on her favorite album, *Blues in the Key of Jazz* by Gemma and the Gemstones. But at 2 a.m., she awoke to the sounds of screams coming from deep in her own throat. She sat bolt upright in bed. Once again, Tommy Whitecraft had come to haunt her dreams.

Chapter 3
The Rebels of Brome County

July 2024

Wild Bill Wallis pulled into the Thirsty Boot on Bolton Pass Road at 8 p.m. He looked around the parking lot but none of the other band members had arrived yet. That made him a little nervous. The gig was at nine and they still had to set up and do a sound check.

But then he remembered: There was a backline at the Boot. Steve Gibson provided equipment for everyone: a Fender Twin-Reverb for Bill on guitar, a Fender Rumble for Augusto on bass; a restored Werner piano for Gemma; and nothing less than a set of Ludwig drums for Stubs. Because of the backline, the band could take their time and arrive about ten minutes before sound check, around eight-thirty. They would be fine. Nothing to worry about. Still, Bill would be more relaxed after his bandmates had all ***arrived***.

He got out of his car, gathered his guitar and pedalboard and locked up the car. He climbed the stairs up to the front patio and entered the Boot through the main door. Inside, through the dim light, he could see that there were already over a dozen people there. Four were sitting at the bar, two couples were playing pool, and the others were seated at various tables throughout. As soon as the door closed behind him, Steve Gibson was there to welcome him.

"Wild Bill," said Steve, "Welcome to the Boot!"

"Hey, Steve," said Bill, "I got just one question for ya."

"Yeah? What's that?"

"Are you ready for the Rebels to rock your world?"

"Goddamn right, I am," said Steve. "I have seventy-eight confirmed and prepaid reservations."

"That's awesome, man," said Bill. "Thanks for all the advanced publicity."

"My pleasure. It's gonna be a helluva night. We are limited only by our legal capacity."

"Oh, and what's that?" asked Bill.

"Well, you see, Bill," Steve said feigning condescension, "that's the maximum number of persons allowed in a bar on any given evening,"

"Very funny, but what's the number?"

"How the hell would I know?" said Steve, "I'm no scientist."

Bill forced a smile and started walking toward the stage, on the far side of the bar.

"Need any help?" asked Steve.

"You already helped enough," said Bill. "You supplied the backline. Nobody supplies a backline."

"We aim to please," said Steve.

Bill had just finished connecting his gear when he heard Gemma St-Onge walk in. The one and only. He smiled. She stopped for a moment to say hello to Steve Gibson then made her way to the stage.

She was dressed all in black flowing robes and scarves, knee-high boots. A veritable rock star. Her hair was fuchsia pink. Gemma sported a different hair color for every gig. Pink, blue, green, red. Sometimes, she wore two colors. However, the mood hit her at the time. Gemma was a superstar but she was no diva, no prima donna. She was kind and considerate to all, especially to fellow musicians. And the crowds loved her. So did Bill. She was a talented singer and an outstanding piano player, classically trained but a total master of all pop music, even jazz.

Bill left his pedals for a moment, stepped down from the stage and went to greet Gemma.

"Wild Bill," she said as he approached.

"Gemma St-Onge," he said. "The legend." He moved in for a hug.

"You are the legend," said Gemma, putting her arms around him. "I'm just the piano player."

"Maybe there's room for two legends," he said.

"We'll make room." she said.

Bill went back to his equipment and Gemma got up on stage, sat at the piano and started to check its tuning, running through the scales from low to high and back again then breaking into piano intros from various pop songs.

When Bill was all set up, he left the stage and went and sat in a chair looking up at Gemma. He could listen to her for hours. He was lucky to have her as part of the band. Audiences loved her and so she was a real draw. In addition to being a phenomenal musician, she was an awesome entertainer who loved working the crowd. She was the life of any party, she lifted any social situation. She was a sincere and authentic human being.

Bill had met her for the first time last year, right here at the Boot, during one of his gigs. The Rebels were a trio back then: Bill, Stubs and Augusto. She was sitting at a table with two other women. During the break, while Bill was making the rounds, chit-chatting with patrons, one of the women at Gemma's table introduced her.

"This is Gemma St-Onge," the woman had said. "Of Gemma and the Gemstones."

Bill had heard of the band but had never heard them play. They were supposed to be very good. They played mostly Sherbrooke, Montreal and Quebec City. Larger venues and music festivals. But never in Knowlton. They were a three-piece band: piano, bass and drums with Gemma doubling on vocals. They played mostly jazz or pop songs with a jazz influence.

"Pleasure to meet you," Bill had said, shaking Gemma's hand.

"Same here," Gemma said.

One of the Gemstones, the drummer, Bill would later learn her name was Lise, stood up and said, "Wild Bill, you should get Gemma to play piano on one of your songs."

Gemma reacted quickly. "No, no, no," she said. "Old piano. Probably not in tune. Not a good idea."

"Gemma," Bill said, "it would be an honor for us to have you sit in. Why don't you check out the piano. If you like it, during the next set, I will invite you up."

"But we came here to drink," said Gemma, pretending to pout, "and to dance, have fun."

But her bandmates urged her on. Bill smiled at their camaraderie. She had to be a great band leader if they loved her this much.

"Okay," she said. "Maybe later."

Bill asked her if there was something in particular she would like to play. Her answer completely floored him. "You tell me what gear you're in, I'll follow you anywhere."

By *gear,* of course, she meant *key.* For a musician, getting up on stage with a band, at the drop of a hat, not knowing what song they would play was an act of bravery. And confidence. That impressed Bill.

Gemma did test the piano and it was in tune, and Bill did call her up during the second set. He chose *Route 66* in the key of G. It was a familiar song to all. It could be drawn out, switching from vocals to solos almost endlessly, and it did not have any chord changes that would be unfamiliar to Gemma.

To no one's surprise and to everyone's delight, the song had been a hit and so was Gemma. What really surprised Bill was that, when the song was over, she got off stage right away, even though her bandmates stood and cheered for her, as did the crowd. Gemma blew kisses to everyone and then stepped down. She knew how to exit gracefully and how not to overstay her welcome. Her ego was totally in check.

Bill was smitten. Professionally speaking, of course. He wanted Gemma in his band. And while Bill and the Rebels played the rest of that set, Bill searched for the words he would use later, to try and entice Gemma to join the Rebels. Even though he could not think of one good reason why an artist the caliber of Gemma St-Onge would want to join a small-time rock 'n roll band.

After the set, he and Gemma went out onto the back deck, overlooking Beaver Pond and talked quietly. Gemma explained that she was honored to be asked to join the band but she already had a band. However, she agreed to sit in any time she was not playing with her Gemstones. Bill was thrilled. The Gemstones didn't play all that often. And she lived in Fulford, so not that far away from any of their gigs.

Bill saw Stubs and Augusto Diaz enter the Boot and heard them exchange niceties with Steve Gibson. Augusto was the quieter of the two, always keeping his greetings short and sweet as he hadn't yet mastered the English language to his liking. At least, that is how he had once explained his reticence to Bill. But Bill found his quiet manner charming especially in contrast to Stubs' boisterousness which could carry great distances and which was not at all in keeping with his diminutive stature. He was about five foot five.

They came walking toward the stage. Stubs had his bag of drum sticks in his hand and Augusto carried his bass in its black rectangular case. They clambered up on stage and Augusto fist-bumped Bill and Gemma. Stubs sat down at the drum kit and began making subtle adjustments to the snare, high-hat, crash cymbals and ride. He hit the kick drum several times. He pulled the high-hat in another inch at which point he seemed happy with the set up.

Augusto tuned up, then plugged into the Rumble and switched on the amp. He started some fingering exercises, running up and down the neck of his bass. There were many styles of bass-playing: walking; slapping; plucking; finger-style; muting. Augusto could do them all. And well.

Bill watched as his musicians prepared. They were such pros. He was thrilled to be working with them. Although, if he was being honest with himself, he had to admit that Stubs was the weakest link. Stubs was the least professional of the four. Bill didn't like thinking in negative terms but a band leader sometimes has to do that. Stubs was a decent enough drummer but he often missed rehearsals, and while never actually late for a gig he often cut it so close that it caused Bill to stress out.

Bill saw Steve Gibson approaching the stage.

"It's almost eight-thirty," said Steve. "Wanna do a sound check now?"

"Let's do it," said Bill.

After sound check, the Rebels made their way to the bar and sat down. Gemma, who was sitting next to Bill, asked, "Did you bring a set list?"

"Oh, yes," he said. "Thanks for reminding me. I'll give it to you when we get back on stage."

Bill looked at Stubs who was also sitting at the bar, texting on his phone. Bill and everyone else knew that Stubs' real job wasn't playing music. It was supplying his clients with their *substance* needs. For the longest time it had been weed but now that grass was legal, he was selling other stuff. Bill wasn't happy about it and told Stubs never to sell at their gigs. Stubs said he wouldn't, but still, he was constantly texting with what Bill presumed were his customers or maybe his suppliers.

A while ago, Bill had to tell Stubs to turn off his phone while on stage. *No distractions*, he had told him. It had been a problem. Bill had often caught Stubs texting on stage between songs. At one point, Bill had to put it to him bluntly. "You have to be all in, Stubs. Totally focused. You're all in or you're all out."

Since that time, Stubs kept his phone off, at least while playing. But right now, he was at the bar.

Now, Stubs waved at Bill. He pointed to his phone and held up two fingers. He was going outside for two minutes. Bill looked at his own phone. It was eight forty-eight. He reluctantly nodded *Okay*. He watched Stubs slip off the bar stool and head out the door.

A few minutes later, at eight fifty-five, Stubs still had not yet returned. Bill went outside to the front patio and looked around the dozen or so tables and chairs but couldn't see him anywhere. There were about ten people out there smoking. Bill hurried to the side of the building. Stubs' red Camaro was in the parking lot, but no Stubs.

Bill took out his phone and speed-dialed his drummer. It went straight to voicemail. There was no point leaving a message. The guy knew where he was supposed to be. Bill went back inside and sat next to Gemma and Augusto while he kept his eyes on the front door. His hand tapped a rhythm on his knee.

At nine sharp, Steve walked up and stood next to Bill and Gemma. "What's happening, guys? We doing this or what?"

Bill looked at Gemma then back at Steve

"We lost Stubs," said Bill

"Stubs died?" asked Steve.

"No, no," said Bill. Sometimes Steve's sense of humor irked Bill. "He's gone. Disappeared."

"I'll check the bathroom," said Steve. "You check outside."

Bill put a hand on Steve's shoulder. "He left. He's gone. We texted, we called. He's gone. But his car is here." He pointed at the stage, now bathed in multi-colored light. "His sticks are still sitting cross-wise on the snare drum."

"Shit," said Steve. "This is not good. Did you guys have a fight? Did he leave in a huff?

"Nope. Nothing like that. He got a text then he got up and left."

Steve looked in the direction of the drum kit and then back at Bill.

"This is not good," said Steve

Bill said, "Gemma and I were just trying to figure out who we can call. To fill in."

"Jesus," said Steve. "Good luck with that. Finding a drummer at this hour? You're supposed to be on stage like . . . now."

"If he doesn't come soon," said Bill, "I think we're going to have to cancel. We can't go on without a drummer. We're a rock band."

"I can't cancel," says Steve. "We've already collected a bunch of money and getting it back to each person could get insane. And canceling can kill a bar's reputation."

"Well, I don't know what else to do, Steve and I'm so sorry. Do you know anyone you can call? Any decent drummer? Nearby?"

"We're short-staffed tonight otherwise I would sit in," said Steve

"You play drums?" said Bill.

"Dude, those are my fucking Ludwigs," said Steve.

"Wow!" said Bill. "Sorry. I didn't know."

"No, no," said Steve. "It's not your fault. I'm sorry. I'm just edgy. I don't like situations like this. Like I said, I'd play but I only have Christina here tonight. She can't handle this crowd alone."

"I'm really sorry," said Bill. "About this whole mess."

"Wait a minute," said Steve. "Maybe Christina's sister can come in. Let me check." Steve held up a finger. "Christina!" he screamed to the woman behind the bar. "*Christina*!" She finally heard him over the din.

"What?"

"Any way Cassandra can work tonight?"

Christina looked shocked. "She just finished at the Pub. She just texted me. She's on her way here. She wanted to know if we needed her."

"Tell her yes!" screamed Steve. "Tell her fucking yes!"

Bill got up and gave Steve a hug. "I'm so sorry, man. We'll make it up to you. I didn't know you played drums."

"Yeah, I do," he said. Then he added, "Where the fuck is Stubs when you need him? I could use a toke right about now. I gotta calm down."

"Augusto," said Bill, "por favor, busca una vez más afuera a nuestro amigo."

"Si, mi amigo," said Augusto, as he rose to go check outside, one last time.

Bill, Gemma and Steve headed for the stage.

Bill turned on his equipment, strapped on his guitar then looked toward the door. Augusto was walking back to the stage shaking his head. *No Stubs.* Cassandra was right behind Augusto. She was wearing a provocatively tight black Tragically Hip T-shirt. She walked to the bar, gave her sister, Christina, a hug and got ready for work. Bill gave Steve, Augusto, and Gemma a copy of the setlist. Each player placed the list on the floor at their feet. Bill stepped up to the mic: "Good evening! We are the Rebels of Brome County!"

They started right off with a strong dance number, a Wild Bill original called "Bolton Pass Blues" and by the time they were halfway through, and while Gemma was doing a piano solo, Bill realized just how good a drummer Steve was. Better than good. He was excellent. He was smooth, calm, and not overly loud. Stubs always had trouble playing softly. Bill had asked him many times to tone it down, especially on ballads. Stubs would try but within a few bars, he was back to pounding hard again. But Steve was another matter. From just this one song, Bill knew that Steve understood nuance.

The Rebels were off and running and running smoothly at that. Bill was thrilled. The second, third, and fourth song went just as smoothly. Through every song, there was a silent communication always going on among the band members. No words. Just glances, smiles and nods of approval. Bill glanced at Steve on drums and received a micro-nod in return. Steve was completely at ease with this kind of communication. He was a pro. He had definitely done this before.

When Gemma was done singing the fourth song, everyone rose and cheered. Gemma was a crowd pleaser. She was an amazing singer and understood instinctively the mood of each song. She was able to convey that mood along with its subtle emotions to the audience. Some pieces were happy and celebratory. Others, sadder and melancholic. And not just the singing. She did the same on the piano. Sometimes, on the more upbeat tunes, she rose and played the piano in a standing position, like Jerry Lee Lewis did in the

1950s. It was no easy feat, because she would have limited access to her pedals. But faster beats, she had once explained to Bill, did not require much pedal work.

The fifth tune on the set list was typically the showstopper. It would feature every member the band in their own solo. It couldn't be a slow song but neither should it be too fast. A medium groove was what Bill preferred because the showstopper was also a dance piece and you didn't want to over-exert the audience. A showstopper tune could go on for ten to fifteen minutes. For this set's showstopper, Bill had chosen an old rock favorite, "Gloria."

As the band played, Bill scanned the crowd, the bar and farther out to see if Stubs might be there, maybe pouting because the band had started without him. But no. No Stubs.

While Steve was doing his drum solo, Bill watched, slightly in awe. Bill hated himself right now because he was thinking what a fine addition Steve would make to the Rebels even though no one yet knew what had actually happened to Stubs.

After they had finished "Gloria," there were less than ten minutes left to the set. The timing was perfect. Bill announced that they would do one more song and then take a short break.

The next song was Bill's "Piledriver," in which Gemma and he shared vocals. That song, with a solo each for Gemma and Bill, should bring them to ten PM. It was also a great dance piece. Not too fast, not too slow.

When "Piledriver" was over and while the crowd applauded, the four musicians thanked them and bowed. Then they congregated near the drums and congratulated Steve on a great set.

"You are amazing, Steve. Simply amazing," said Bill. Augusto and Gemma whole-heartedly agreed.

"Well," said Steve. "I don't know about *amazing. Outstanding* maybe."

Bill grabbed Steve by the shoulder. "Come on. Let me buy you a beer."

They laughed, left the stage and made their way to the bar.

But first, Bill navigated his way through the crowd and headed for the front door. He needed a bit of fresh air. And he was a little worried about what to do if Stubs showed up now that this first set was over. He wanted to finish the gig with Steve, damn it! His mind was made up. Even if Stubs did show up, they would finish with Steve. Stubs could go home for all he cared.

Outside, Bill surveyed the small crowd out on the patio, smoking and looking happy. No Stubs. He looked to the side of the building. The red Camaro was still there.

When Bill got back to the bar, a beer was waiting for him. Steve slid it over.

"Hey," said Bill. "I was supposed to buy *you* a beer."

Steve pointed across the bar. "That fellow just bought us a round."

Bill turned. "Plaid shirt?" he asked.

"Black dress shirt," said Steve. "Good-looking guy."

Bill saw the fellow and lifted his glass in thanks. The guy acknowledged. The guy was indeed good-looking, distractingly so, and about the same age as Bill. His hair was neatly cropped and he looked very fit. The second button on his black shirt was undone but the shirt was not open. That would have been tacky. Standing at the bar, he seemed maybe an inch taller than Bill. Bill decided to walk over and say Hi.

"Thanks for the drinks," said Bill.

"Thanks for the great music," said the guy. "And a great show."

"We have another set for you," said Bill. "So, don't leave just yet. I'm Bill Wallis, by the way." Bill extended a hand.

"I know who you are, Wild Bill." said the stranger, as they shook hands. "I'm Finn Toomey. I like your music. You guys are great. Hey, but where's Stubs tonight?"

"He had to leave before the gig started. We were lucky to have Steve Gibson fill in." As Bill spoke, he noticed that Finn's eyes diverted slightly over Bill's right shoulder. Bill turned to see what Finn might be looking at. It was Cassandra and her Tragically Hip T-shirt. She was reaching for beer glasses on the upper shelf, above the bar, and everyone sitting at the bar or within eyeshot seemed captivated by her ever-emerging midriff.

"Nice to meet you, Finn," said Bill as he turned and walked back to the bar.

At ten-twenty the band was gathering at the stage, readying for their second and final set. Steve walked up to Bill and asked, "You want me up there again?"

"Hell, yes," said Bill. "You up for it?"

"For sure, man," said Steve.

They started their second set with another Wild Bill composition: "Dance All Night. Bill set up the tempo with just chords, just four bars, and with that, the rest of the band came in. It was a song that people loved dancing to. He had written the song as an exercise with his English Lit students at Massey-Vanier High School. Each student had to write a verse. They had all loved the exercise. He'd brought an acoustic guitar to class and they had all sung their verses while he strummed the chords. But this final version had verses that only Bill had written. Of course, it wasn't Tennyson or Yeats, but audiences liked it. Bill began singing:

Working all week just to pay the bills / Friday night comes and it's time to chill

We're gonna dance all night (the band repeated)

We're gonna dance all night (the band repeated)

We're gonna dance all night, dance until the break of dawn

He sang a second verse and then called on Gemma for a solo. When she was finished, he resumed singing.

Everyone here dressed up mighty fine / drinking their beer or sipping on wine

We're gonna dance all night (the band repeated)

We're gonna dance all night (the band repeated)

We're gonna dance all night, dance until the break of dawn

Bill sang another verse and then called on Augusto for a bass solo after which Bill resumed singing.

The Thirsty Boot is where we kick up our heels / come on baby, you know how it feels

We're gonna dance all night (the band repeated)

We're gonna dance all night (the band repeated)

We're gonna dance all night, dance until the break of dawn

They were coming to the end of the song. Bill took a lengthy guitar solo while moving wirelessly about the stage. He then left the stage and continued soloing while joining the dancers on the floor. Half the people were dancing and the others were standing watching him play, making his guitar cry and scream.

When he was done soloing and he was back at his mic, he sang the closing verse one last time and at the very end, he held up the neck of his guitar and when he brought it down, the band brought the song to a loud, crashing end.

From there, they did three more dance songs and then moved on to a Gemma original: "Emotional Shrapnel." It was a ballad but still had a quiet danceability to it and so some people chose to do just that. But mostly, people gathered around the stage, near the piano, to watch Gemma play and to listen to her sing. If you were standing in front of Gemma when she performed, you felt that it was all for you, especially if she looked directly at you when she sang. The experience could be mesmerizing.

Strangely though, Gemma never sang to men or made eye contact with them when she sang. Only with women. It was her experience, she had once explained to Bill, that if a man thought she was singing to him, he would interpret it as *She wants me* and he might come around after the set, lingering like some love-struck lapdog. That was not the case with women. Women were able to connect with other women on levels that men simply could not fathom. Gemma could sing to women and they would just soar and explore the emotions and not jump to silly, sexual conclusions. Women could hug each other or hold hands. Hell, they could even sleep in the same bed and it would not be sexual. Men were incapable of such things. Bill envied that capacity in women and often wondered why the two genders were so dissimilar in that regard. Was it nature? Was it our upbringing? Had society imposed these limitations upon the genders? Upon men? Or did it go deeper, he wondered? He had no idea.

Bill was fortunate to have been brought up with five sisters. No brothers. And he was the youngest sibling. His sisters' influence on him was undeniable and he loved them dearly. As children, his sisters had never changed their behavior when Bill was around. They totally welcomed him into their world, treated him like one of the girls, and he had reveled in it. Maybe that was why, even today, he felt more comfortable in the company of women than he did with men. Maybe that was why he got along so well with Gemma. To Bill, Gemma was like a sister as well as a dear friend and musical collaborator.

Sometimes, Bill felt that he had been cheated. Maybe he would have been happier if he had been born a female. But he did not do well with men. He did not like discussing cars, hunting, sports, or other male-centered minutiae that most guys prattled on about. He was attracted to men but didn't like them. He loved women but was not drawn to them. Not in that way.

Who the hell was he? What the hell was he? Were there not enough letters out there for Bill to find himself? He googled it every once in a while. LGBTQ was now LGBTQIA2S? And in all that inclusion he struggled to find a place for himself. G was for *gay* but that was not all he was. Q was not only *queer*, it also referred to *questioning*. Sure, that fit him but so what. The *I* and *A* referred to *intersexual* and *asexual*. He didn't identify as that at all. *2S* stood for *two spirits*. Well, okay, but again, what did that mean for his life choices? Where would he find his happiness? Celebrities all over the world, even sports figures were now "coming out". But if Bill came out, what would he come out as? Maybe add a new letter to the list: C for confused. That sounded more like a Sue Grafton novel than acknowledgment of one's sexual identity. Soon, he would be turning thirty and still he did not really know himself.

In a way, it was the same in his life as a musician. People often complimented him on his talent as a guitarist. They would say that he sounded exactly like Eric Clapton, Stevie Ray Vaughn, David

Gilmour or Jimi Hendrix. He had indeed spent many years practicing trying to master the respective sounds of his musical heroes but what was his sound? What was his own voice on guitar? He had no idea. He felt inauthentic, an imposter. On guitar and in his personal life. He wondered if some day he'd come into his own, to know for sure that he was actually good at something.

Luckily though, Bill had been fortunate enough to have a father who had served as an excellent role model. His dad had always acted like a man but never macho, and he was kind and respectful to his houseful of females. If not for his father's influence and the great dignity the man had, Bill felt that he might have worn his confused sexuality on his sleeve, as it were. That would have proven awkward growing up. Even disastrous. His father, without realizing it, had taught Bill how to navigate both worlds; that of men and that of women without having to reveal his secret torment. *Secret Torment,* thought Bill. That would make a great title for one of Gemma's songs. Not Bill's. Bill wrote songs that were typically superficial. Good dance numbers and fun for everyone, but a little on the shallow side. But Gemma: She was the queen of profundity.

And now, as Gemma sang one final time, the chorus to "Emotional Shrapnel," Bill scanned the crowd, the chairs, the floor beyond the bar, where the pool table was and the entrance. The place seemed weirdly marked by absence: no Stubs.

Bill wasn't sure what to feel. Of course, he was angry with Stubs for disappearing just before the gig but he pulled back on that emotion because he also felt some concern. What the hell happened to him? Where did he go? Bill didn't want to lock in on any one emotion until he knew exactly what had occured.

The rest of the set went quickly. It seemed to whizz by. And now, for the last song of the night, Bill had chosen Eric Clapton's "Layla," the original electric version of course. He introduced the song simply with his guitar. The opening riff was so recognizable that everyone was immediately up and on the floor, either dancing or watching. For the band, for Bill at least, it was a magnificent high. Nothing compared to connecting with a crowd like this. The feeling was indescribable. They all felt it. Gemma looked over at Bill and smiled. They all exchanged glances. This is what it was all about.

At four minutes in, the song went into its second, mellower part, and now Gemma was featured on piano. Again, people gathered closer to Gemma. Rather than dance, they just swayed to the music, watching her play. She was the most captivating musician Bill had ever played with. And with this second part of "Layla", the Rebels let the crowd down easy, letting them know the end was near. Soon, they would have to go home.

When the song came to an end with a loud burst of instrumentation, Bill raised his guitar with its neck high, signaling the band to hold the final notes. When he brought his guitar down, they stopped in unison. Again the crowd cheered, whistled and applauded.

Bill stepped to the mic: "There is no audience like a Thirsty Boot audience. You guys were great tonight and thank you!"

Everyone applauded and the band bowed. They put down their instruments, turned off the amps and slowly headed for the bar, walking among and chatting with audience members as they went.

It was eleven forty-five. Bill sat down at the bar and checked his phone while Gemma, Augusto and Steve gathered around him.

"Any news?" asked Gemma.

"No," said Bill. "No texts, no voicemail. Nothing."

"Mierde, " said Augusto.

"I'm going outside to look around," said Bill.

There were at least a dozen people on the front patio, smoking and chatting.

"Great show!" said a guy with long scraggly hair, sticking out from underneath a ratty Montreal Expos ball cap. Two of his friends reached out and touched Bill on the shoulder as he passed by. "Great job, Wild Bill," said one.

Bill said thanks and went down the stairs to the parking lot. Stubs' Camaro was still there. He checked around the car and even peered inside. The rear windows were heavily tinted, impossible to see through but on the front passenger seat, Bill saw the AC/DC ball cap that Stubs wore everywhere, except on gigs. Stubs must have left with someone else. There was no other possibility. He climbed the stairs back up to the patio and went inside to Gemma, Augusto and Steve.

"Car's still there," he said. "This is getting weird."

"Dangerous business he's in," said Steve, saying what Bill was also thinking but unwilling to say out loud.

They sat for a while at the bar, sipping their beers and watching people slowly leaving the Boot. Bill glanced over every time the door opened to see if Stubs might walk in, with some lame excuse. Like the ones he gave for missing rehearsals: *My dog was sick; my dad needed help changing the hot water tank; my car wouldn't start; I fell asleep watching* Jeopardy. He had missed many rehearsals. Missing a rehearsal wasn't the end of the world. The band could still work on things they were developing. But it still irked Bill something awful. Rehearsals were for the whole band. Curiously, for a guy who spent so much time on his phone, Stubs never bothered to call or text that he wouldn't be at rehearsal.

But Stubs was a good drummer. Not great, but competent. And decent drummers were hard to find. For some time now, Bill had been keeping his ears open for potential replacements, to no avail. But with tonight's incident, Bill's mind was almost made up. He needed to find a new drummer.

At midnight, Bill said, "I think it's time to go home."

"I agree," said Gemma.

"Thanks again, Steve," said Bill, "for a great gig. You were amazing."

Steve nodded enthusiastically. "Man, it was a great night. And I haven't had so much fun in a long time. You guys are super tight. And I hope Stubs is okay."

Bill and Augusto grabbed their gear and, along with Gemma, made their way to the front door.

"Let me know what happens," said Steve.

"You bet. For sure I will," said Bill.

As they walked toward the door, Bill fought the urge to turn and ask Steve if he might consider joining the Rebels. That would be premature. It would also be wrong. Bill had to find out what happened to Stubs first. If Stubs was okay and had no good excuse for having bailed on them, Bill would have every right to think about replacing him. But if something bad had happened to Stubs . . . well . . . first things first. Plus there was no guarantee that Steve would want to join the rebels. Or *could* join the rebels. Running the Thirsty Boot was surely a full-time job. The Rebels played most weekends and Steve was at the Boot most weekends.

When Bill, Gemma and Augusto stepped outside onto the front patio, they stopped dead in their tracks. They saw a tow truck, with lights flashing, in the parking lot. The driver was in the process of hooking up the red Camaro. Next to the tow truck was an SQ police car. Bill watched as a uniformed police officer climbed the stairs to the deck. Only one. The other officer stayed with the tow truck driver. Upon seeing the approaching police officer, the few customers who were still on the front deck, slowly took their leave.

The cop was a woman. A female police officer. Bill had never met one before. She approached the band members. She looked all business. She was tall, with dirty blond hair in a ponytail and she addressed them in French.

"Parlez-vous français . . . anglais?" she asked.

Bill looked around. "We are all bilingual," he said. "But I guess we prefer English?" *Oh, my God,* he thought. Did he just use upspeak? He hated that. Ending a declarative sentence as though it were a question. *Shame on you.*

"Do you know who that car belongs to?" she asked, pointing with her thumb toward the Camaro.

"Yes," said Bill. He could hear his own voice quivering slightly. "It belongs to our drummer, Stubs."

"Stubs?" she repeated.

"Sorry. Wayne Lacroix," said Bill. "Is he okay? I have to talk to him?"

"I'm Corporal Alison," said the cop. "Can we sit down?" She pointed to the table and chairs next to them.

All patrons had left the deck at this point. The Rebels were alone with Corporal Alison. They all sat down.

"May I ask your names?" she asked.

"I'm Bill Wallis." Bill spelled out his family name.

"Gemma St-Onge."

"Augusto Diaz."

Corporal Alison wrote in her notebook.

"What's going on?" said Bill. "Where's Stubs?"

Corporal Alison looked up from her notebook. "At about 10 p.m. we received a call from a resident on Tuer Road, not far from here. They reported a suspicious car next to the church. And some suspicious activity. When we arrived at the scene, next to the church, we found a body. No one else. No car."

"A body?" said Bill.

Corporal Alison nodded. "Yes. It was Wayne Lacroix."

"No!" said Bill emphatically. "He was here tonight. We had a beer together."

Gemma reached out and put her hand on Bill's arm. Then Gemma spoke to Corporal Alison.

"He was murdered, wasn't he?" said Gemma.

Corporal Alison nodded. "Yes. I'm very sorry to say that. I can't tell you much right now but it looks that way."

"What the fuck happened? said Bill.

Again, Gemma touched Bill's arm.

"Please, Corporal," said Gemma. "Tell us what you can."

"He was shot," the officer said simply. "I'm sorry."

Bill, Gemma and Augusto looked at each other.

Corporal Alison drew a circle with her index finger in the direction of the three of them. "You three were here all evening?"

"Yes, all night," said Bill. "We're the band. Stubs is our drummer."

"He must have left at one point," said Corporal Alison.

"He arrived at around eight-thirty," said Bill, but around five to nine, he said he was going outside for a few minutes. He never came back."

"Did he say why he was leaving?"

"He got a text message," said Bill. "He pointed to his phone and said he was going outside for a minute."

Corporal Alison nodded and wrote in her notebook. She then turned back to Bill. "He has an address in Bondville," she said. "Do you think that is his current address?"

"Yes," said Bill. "That's where he lives. In Bondville. On Blackwood Street. I forget the number."

The corporal wrote in her notebook.

"Does he live with someone?" the cop asked. "Wife, girlfriend . . . roommate?"

"No," said Bill. "It's a small house. He lives alone. He has a dog. I know he has family in Waterloo. His mom and dad, but I don't know them. I mean I never met them."

Bill looked at Gemma and Augusto. They shook their heads. They had never met Stubs' family either.

Holy crap, thought Bill. This was real. Stubs was dead. He would never see Stubs again. Stubs would never play drums with the Rebels again. He was gone. Gone forever. And now, all those negative thoughts that Bill had had all evening, about Stubs, about his drumming, about his tardiness, about how it might be time to look for a replacement, all of those words came rushing back in a tsunami of guilt.

Just then Steve Gibson came outside. He saw the Rebels sitting at the table with the cop. They were all silent. No one was talking.

"Hell," said Steve, smirking. "Who died?"

"I'm Corporal Alison," said the cop, standing up and holding out her right hand.

They shook.

Steve's smile was fading fast. "What's going on? I'm Steve Gibson. I own the place."

Corporal Alison wrote in her notebook. "Can you sit with us?" she asked.

Steve sat down, glancing at the Rebels.

"Wayne Lacroix has been found dead," she said.

Steve had a puzzled look on his face. He turned to Bill.

Bill looked at Steve. "Stubs," he said, "his name is . . . was Wayne Lacroix."

Bill turned back to Corporal Alison. "Steve filled in on drums tonight. Because Stubs wasn't here."

"What happened?" asked Steve

"He was shot," said Corporal Alison.

"Jesus Christ," said Steve.

"So," said Corporal Alison, "Someone must have come to pick him up. At about eight fifty-five?

They all looked at each other shrugging yet agreeing.

Corporal Alison focused her gaze on Steve. "How many people did you have here tonight?"

"At least one twenty-five," said Steve, clearly relieved to say a number under the legal limit. "Seventy-eight prepaid."

"What's your capacity?" she asked.

"One-fifty," said Steve.

"Could you give us a list of those people with their contact info?"

"The people who prepaid, yes, no problem at all," said Steve. "Are you thinking that one of my customers had something to do with this?"

"No, no," she said. "But maybe someone saw something. Maybe saw who came and picked up Lacroix. If anyone contacts you and says they saw something, please have them call me?" She gave Steve a card. And then, almost as an afterthought, she gave each of the band members a card as well.

"Jojo Alison," Steve said, looking at the card then at the officer. "Corporal." He placed the card in his shirt pocket.

"I need a favor from all of you," said the Corporal. "I need you to wait here for about a half-hour. Homicide investigators are on their way. They will want to talk to you. Is that okay?"

They all nodded okay.

"Again," she said. "I am very sorry for your loss."

She looked at Steve and pointed to the door. "Do you have bottled water in there?"

"Yes," he said.

"Please?" she asked.

"I'll be right back," said Steve, getting up. Then he looked at the rest of the group. "Anyone else?"

They all looked at each other and shook their heads *no*. Steve went inside.

Gemma spoke up. "Corporal Alison, may I ask you a question?"

"Yes."

Looking at the business card the corporal had given her moments earlier, Gemma said, "Your name is Jojo Alison. Are you any relation to Joanna Alison, the author?"

"Yes," said the corporal. "She is my mother."

"I thought so," said Gemma, smiling softly. "I've read all your mom's books. She dedicates each book to you and your dad, doesn't she?"

"Yes," said the corporal, almost smiling. "She does."

"And your dad is a police officer as well?" said Gemma.

"Was," said the corporal. "He's retired now."

"I have all her books," said Gemma. "I've read them all. Even the most recent: *Runaway*. Please tell your mom that you met a fan tonight."

"I will."

Gemma hesitated. "May I ask you another question?"

The corporal nodded.

"This must be the most terrible part of your job," said Gemma. "Notifying people that their loved one has died?"

Corporal Alison seemed both touched and slightly surprised at the question. She nodded.

"And it will be even harder, won't it?" said Gemma, "when you have to meet with Wayne's family?"

"Yes," said the corporal. "These are very sad situations. But the homicide investigators may choose to notify the next of kin themselves."

"Still, I do not envy you your job, Corporal Alison," said Gemma. "It must take a terrible toll on you. I mean I can't even begin to imagine the emotional shrapnel."

Bill caught that. Gemma had just cited the title of one of her own songs.

"There are parts of this job," said Corporal Alison, "that are very difficult. But there are some very positive aspects as well. Sometimes we do good things for people. We get to help. That can be very rewarding."

The door to the Boot opened and Steve emerged. He handed Corporal Alison her water. She thanked him and handed him a five-dollar bill. Steve put up a hand and said it wasn't necessary but she insisted and thanked him again.

Bill saw the door open again and this time Cassandra emerged, walking hand-in-hand with that good-looking guy who had bought the band a round of beer earlier. Finn *something*. Corporal Alison's eyes locked on the guy. The guy, seeing the cop there, let go of Cassandra's hand which Bill found extremely strange. Since when was holding hands a crime? Corporal Alison kept her eyes on the couple until they had made their way across the patio and down the steps to the parking lot.

"That's Cassandra," said Steve. "Cassandra Dudley. Cassandra and her sister, Christina, worked the bar tonight."

"Dudley," repeated Corporal Alison, writing in her notebook.

"I don't know the guy's name," said Steve

"It's okay," said Corporal Alison. "I know his name." Then asked, "Was that guy here all evening?"

"I don't know," said Steve. "I was playing drums most of the night. I was not in any position to keep tabs on anyone."

"I understand," said Corporal Alison. Then she added, "Mr. Gibson, any chance you have security cameras here?"

"Two inside. That's it. Nothing outside. It's on my to-do list. Sorry"

"That's okay," she said. "Can I get a copy of what you have?"

Steve got up. "Sure, I'll get that for you right now."

Corporal Alison thanked him and took a long drink of her water. She checked her cell phone then turned to the group. "Investigators are not far. They'll be here soon. They've asked me not to talk about the case. They will want to talk to you."

Everyone nodded. No one knew what to say. There was an awkward silence.

Bill noticed that the tow truck was finally leaving with Stubs' red Camaro up on the bed. They had taken unusual care of the car, slowly winching it up onto the flatbed. It was evidence. The cop who had been with the tow truck driver came up the stairs to the patio. He nodded to Corporal Alison then sat down at the next table. He gave Bill and his companions a once-over but his eyes lingered a while on Gemma.

Corporal Alison told the officer that the investigators were on their way and he nodded in acknowledgement.

Corporal Alison took another sip from her water. "Did you all have a good show tonight?" she asked.

Bill presumed that the cop was just making small talk now, while waiting for investigators to arrive, having been forbidden by them to speak of the case.

"Yes, but it was strange not having Stubs here," said Bill. "We were worried about him."

"I understand," said Corporal Alison.

Steve came back out and handed Corporal Alison a thumb drive. "It's all there, as of five this afternoon."

"Thank you," she said, putting it into her shirt pocket.

The silence resumed, but then Corporal Alison turned to Gemma. "I know this is a bad time but may I ask *you* a question now?"

Gemma, a little taken aback, said yes.

"You are Gemma of Gemma and the Gemstones, aren't you?"

Gemma said that she was.

Corporal Alison turned her chair toward Gemma, leaning in just a little.

"I know this is a bad time," said the corporal, "And I'm so sorry but I saw you, with the Gemstones, live, several times. Once at the JazzFest in Montreal. You are my favorite band ever. I love your music. You and the Gemstones. I follow you on Facebook. I try never to miss a show. I have all of your music."

All eyes were on Corporal Alison and she must have felt it.

"I'm sorry," she said. "I know this is a bad time. A sad time. I'm very sorry."

Now Gemma looked around at the others. She was blushing.

"Well," said Gemma, "thank you for the kind words, corporal. And when I'm not playing with the Gemstones, I play with the Rebels." She raised her palm gently, toward Bill and Augusto.

The corporal turned to Bill. "And are the Rebels on Facebook?"

"Yes," said Bill. "We are. Search for The Rebels of Brome County."

"Then I will follow the Rebels on Facebook," said Corporal Alison, turning back to Gemma, "so that I might see you at another show. If that would be okay."

Gemma beamed. "That would be most excellent. If I see you, I will play a song just for you."

"Oh, please," said Corporal Alison, raising her hand slightly. "Don't do that. I would be so embarrassed."

"Oh, no one would know," said Gemma. "I would be very discreet. Only you and I would know."

"Still," said the corporal. "I don't think so."

"Oh but, Corporal," said Gemma, leaning in just a little, "you have not lived until someone has sung a song for you. Just for you."

Now it was Corporal Alison's turn to blush.

Gemma turned to Bill. "May I share the good news?" she asked.

Bill nodded.

Gemma turned back to Corporal Alison. "We will all be playing at the Brome Fair in August. Both bands. The Gemstones and the Rebels. It's a first. We are so excited about that."

"That is great news," said Corporal Alison. "In fact, I too will be working Brome Fair this year. All weekend."

"Oh, my," said Gemma, putting her palms together and sitting back. "Then I will immediately begin thinking about which song I'll sing to you."

Corporal Alison nervously reached for her mobile phone on her belt. She had received a text message.

"The investigators are in Knowlton," she said. "They'll be here any moment now."

Chapter 4
The Scourge of Stagecoach Road

Part I
In the Beginning

In Cormac McCarthy's *No Country for Old Men*, veteran Sheriff Ed Tom Bell bemoans the evil forces he sees "coming down the pike." They are unlike anything he has seen before and he has dealt with some evil people. The lawman feels not so much unable as unwilling to become what he would have to become in order to confront this new menace, this new form of criminality. He feels that doing so might "put his soul at hazard." Consequently, he questions his future as a peace officer. He then goes on to tell the story of this "true and living prophet of destruction" which has brought him to a crossroads in life. That story is set in 1980.

This story is set in 1976. And unlike the good Sheriff in Cormac McCarthy's work, what I see "coming down the pike" are hopes for safer and improved communities and civilization. The madness and mayhem, the lawlessness and recklessness of the late 1970s, I see as things receding in the rearview mirror. Stay with me, dear reader, right till the end of this story. See if you agree.

My name is Alistair MacKenzie and I am a retired reporter from a prominent Anglo newspaper based in Sherbrooke, Quebec, a newspaper which shall remain nameless for reasons I will get into in a moment. I worked there for over thirty-five years at the police desk, covering stories of crime and justice in the erstwhile Brome County. Naturally, my job was to report on petty crimes as well as some downright violent and bizarre atrocities. During those years I had the honor and privilege of meeting some of the county's finest people and to tell their stories.

There was one story, though, that I researched and wrote and rewrote several times that was never published. That is why I do not wish to disclose the name of the newspaper. My editor killed the story. He claimed it wasn't sufficiently substantiated. I understood his position, but the people who I interviewed refused to go on record although they did swear to the veracity of the facts and they actually corroborated the versions that others had put forth. That story has stuck with me all these years and today, now that all the people involved are dead and gone, I think the time is right to tell it.

This is a story as told to me by people of Brome County and especially of Brome Village. This is their story. Not mine. Again, I have every confidence that what they told me is solidly true.

I must also acknowledge my myriad conversations with my dearly departed friend and drinking buddy, Jacques Latendresse. Jacques was an SQ police officer during the time that I worked as a reporter. He had served as a patrol officer and then as an investigator at the Cowansville detachment. Often, at the end of our day's work, we would end up at the Hotel Yamaska in Cowansville where we would drink beer, play pool and swap stories. I gained much of what I know about the inside subtleties and workings of the SQ from Jacques.

We are talking about the old Brome County, not the current MRC of Brome-Missisquoi. At the time, Brome County extended further than it does now. It extended as far as Mansonville and Highwater to the southeast and almost to Magog, more precisely Bishop Road on the northeast and ended at West Brome to the west.

And this was right around the time (1971) that the town of Knowlton merged with Bondville, Fulford, Foster, Iron Hill, West Brome and East Hill to form the Town of Brome Lake. Today, if you were to look at a map of the Town of Brome Lake you would see that there is a slice missing from the southern portion, the bottom part. That slice is Brome Village, home of the annual Big Brome Fair as it was known then, which was and still is, the largest agricultural exposition in Quebec having its roots going back to the 1850s, when the town was known as Brome Corners and when Stagecoach Road was the main thoroughfare between St-Jean and Knowlton's Landing. The citizens of Brome Village wanted nothing to do with that 1971 merger and voted it down. They wanted nothing to do with the increase in taxes that would inevitably ensue. They just wanted to be themselves and be on their own, like they had been doing since the 1850s. There was a rebellious spirit that existed in Brome Village which is still alive today. I love that spirit. I love the people of Brome Village. Personally, I live in Austin (formerly in Brome County) and my family has been here for six generations and continues to thrive here. But I have always maintained that if I were to live anywhere else in this world, it would be Brome Village. I love that town.

The police, at the time, as it is today, was the Sûreté du Québec. The SQ was located in the city of Cowansville, but around 1975 they moved to a location on Dunham Road, on Highway 202. Just recently, in 2024, they moved to a larger facility on the same road but closer to Cowansville.

The SQ covered all of Brome and Missisquoi counties which extended from the Richelieu River near Noyan in the west to Lake Memphremagog to the east and from Autoroute 10 in the north to the US border in Vermont in the south. Given this vast expanse, it could easily take close to an hour for a patrol officer to travel from one end of the territory to the other, for example, from Clarenceville to Highwater.

Also contributing to the policing services in Brome County during this time, was the newly formed police force for the Town of Brome Lake. The former Knowlton police department had been expanded and renamed and now patrolled the communities that comprised the new municipality. In 2002, the Town of Brome Lake Police disbanded whereupon the SQ took over and it continues to this day.

For the SQ, in the 1970s, there were normally two or three police cars, occasionally four, on a given shift, covering both Brome and Missisquoi counties. However, it happened frequently that due to staff shortages, court duty, and so on, only one car was available to serve both counties. And it was not uncommon that the farther reaches of the territory, those towns most distant from the detachment in Cowansville, could go without police presence for long periods of time. Essentially, in those days, it was common for citizens of Mansonville, Austin, and Brome Village to not even see a police car for weeks. Moreover, as one might expect, the SQ concentrated their patrols on the major highways such as the 139, 104 and the 202.

Brome County of the mid-1970s was not what it is today. Yes, there were cottage-goers but they were fewer in number compared to today and they generally kept to themselves. And the tourism industry of today was virtually non-existent at that time. So, if you were out and about in any of Brome County's towns, you normally met only locals. Brome County was a rural area. And the main pastime for many of its residents, aside from working their day-to-day jobs, was drinking.

Every town had its watering hole, and they were mostly called hotels. But the renting of rooms was never a priority for them. Their stock in trade was alcohol, beer mostly. There was the Mansonville Hotel, the Bolton Center Hotel, the Hotel Gilmore at Gilman's Corner, the Prince of Wales Hotel in Abercorn. the Brome Hotel in Brome Village, the Owl's Nest Inn and the Shaggy Dog in South Bolton. The Town of Brome Lake, all by itself, had its fair share: the Foster Hotel which locals ironically referred to as the Hilton, a small bar below what is now the Auberge Le Relais that locals called the Snake Pit, and the Terrasse Inn in Bondville. There was also the Knowlton Pub and the Thirsty Boot on Bolton Pass Road, both of which are still in operation today. I am not proud to report that I was on a first-name basis with most of the owners of these establishments, but that fact did serve me well documenting the details that I share with the reader in this story.

Each community's drinking spot had their patrons, their regulars, who were there every weekend and often during the week as well. Fights were a common occurrence in these establishments and, from time to time, these patrons would, having grown tired of brawling among themselves and being thoroughly liquored up, decide to leave their hometown and go challenge the patrons of the hotel in a neighboring town. For example, the ruffians of the Prince of Wales, when there were no Americans from Vermont to pick on, would pile into their pickup trucks and head north to the Gilmore and pick a fight with the drinkers there who were only too happy to oblige. Mansonville malcontents would drive to Bolton Centre or to Knowlton. In fact, it was not uncommon for revelers from more distant jurisdictions to come to Brome County to flex their muscle. For example, bikers from Granby often came all the way to Knowlton to test their Francophone mettle against that of the Anglos. Again, this was the 1970s. Brome County was predominantly Anglophone.

Now, the reader might very well wonder, weren't these ne'er-do-wells afraid of being stopped for impaired driving? Well, no, not really. True, the breathalyzer had recently come into use and convictions for the offense had increased. But drunk driving was not the crime it is today. The worst you were looking at if you hadn't killed someone in an accident, was a fine. For example, it was typical for a judge to condemn a person who had tested double the legal limit of point 08 to a concomitant $160 fine. No jail time, no suspended drivers' permit. Times were different then. Also, as mentioned earlier, the police had to be lucky enough to be on site to even spot a drunk driver, let alone arrest one.

Traffic violations were equally low in consequence. Almost all offenses were met with a $27 fine. A really serious driving infraction would have to be charged under the Criminal Code of Canada, for example, for Dangerous Driving.

Now, most bar fights usually didn't last long. They fizzled out relatively quickly. They rarely lasted over a minute or less. I imagine it's pretty much the same today, but what do I know about bar fights in this day and age? I stopped drinking in 2000 and haven't been around alcohol except for the occasional wedding or wake, the former of which we see far too few today and the latter, more than I like. But I digress. So, the fight was usually over in short order, one person having bested the other with a sucker punch or a well-timed kick to the groin. Only rarely would a full-fledged brawl break out involving a large group of patrons. These were called bench-clearers, after the hockey tradition. Again, very rare.

And the hotel owners or bouncers, at the first sign of any kind of a squabble, quickly escorted the aggrieved parties outdoors to conclude their discussions in the parking lot. The owners did not want any damage to their lavish furnishings. I'm being sarcastic, of course. Most hotels were very moderately decorated and furnished, some were complete dumps.

And rarely were the police even called. An even rarer occurrence was for someone to actually want to make a complaint to the police and have someone charged with assault. Police might offer but it just wasn't done. You took your licks and shut up about it and maybe planned a revenge match at a future date. Occasionally a stranger or tourist who had insulted a local and had received a physical comeuppance wanted to file a complaint. But those incidents usually led nowhere.

Usually, by the time the police arrived at the scene of any of these dust-ups, it was all over or it had spilled out into the parking lot and as soon as they saw the police arrive, it was definitely over and everyone was friends again.

In the event of the rare bench-clearer, the hotel owner might decide to call the SQ to come and quell the disturbance. But the SQ were in no hurry to do that. The officers of Cowansville detachment, who patrolled a large territory, would take their time responding to any disturbance in a hotel. They had learned early on that if they did arrive at the hotel while the melee was still in full swing, they might easily be drawn into the fracas, risking life and limb to these drunken hooligans who vastly outnumbered them and who would be thrilled to make the claim that they had punched out an active-duty cop. Furthermore, the SQ officers were essentially on their own, even if they were two to a car after 8 p.m. Back-up or reinforcements were hard to find and anyway, they would have to travel from Granby, Marieville or Sherbrooke each over an hour away.

So, the unwritten rule for the SQ was to take your time. If you were smart, you arrived when the ruckus was over, to clean up the mess and write a quick occurrence report. If the hotel owner complained about the SQ's tardiness, they were told to hire more bouncers. Bouncers was the vernacular of the day. Today, they might call them doormen, security people or assistant managers.

And as if this were not enough hooliganism for the small towns of Brome County, there emerged from among their numbers certain individuals who stood out above the rest. And not in a good way. They were so notorious, so insanely crazy and ruthless and pugilistic that they were in a category all their own. Almost every town had at least one of these anti-heroes, these miscreants. From Austin, to Mansonville to West Brome, there were some despicable and downright wicked men.

Bolton Centre had Anthony (Tony) Curtis who was no relation to the movie star of the era although some locals claimed he did bear a resemblance to the handsome movie star. Mansonville had Phil Lachapelle. Abercorn had Alan Sherrer. They were the alpha males in communities already heavily invested in alphas. These were the kind of people who would not only pick a fight with you if you looked at them crosswise, but they might pick a fight even if you didn't look at them. Because they were so drunk, paranoia often got the better of them and they would see insult where none was intended.

Phil Lachapelle did that exact thing one night at the Mansonville Hotel. He was sitting with a few cronies when he became obsessed with a stranger sitting at the bar who was staring at him. Phil apparently took the stranger for one of those rich, arrogant city people who probably had a cottage on Lake Memphremagog and who, although he was in a bar, still wore his sunglasses, like a movie star or celebrity. The situation ate at Phil for several minutes until he couldn't take it anymore. He got up, walked around the bar, pushed the guy off his stool and proceeded to rough him up which was no easy task given that the stranger's seeing-eye dog was biting at Phil's left leg the whole time. The police were called for that incident and the stranger did indeed want his attacker charged. Phil Lachapelle ended up serving three months for the assault.

Our Bolton Center anti-hero, Tony Curtis was once arrested and charged when he came home after a night of heavy drinking and proceeded to beat up a family of four who had broken into his home and who were watching television in his living room. The only problem was that it wasn't Curtis' home. So blind drunk was he that he had entered *their* home by mistake. He was arrested, charged, and served two months in jail. Luckily, no one was seriously injured.

These super-thugs were all bullies, drunks and petty thieves. All had been charged and convicted of a variety of offenses in their communities and all had served at least some time in jail. It was an era of rebels and outlaws. My friend, Jacques Latendresse, was fond of comparing Brome County to the Far West. *Gang de Bandits*, he would say. *Des hosties de cowboys! C'est pas possible.* These were wild times indeed.

Part II
The Scourge of Stagecoach Road

And so, into this quiet and idyllic rural setting of Brome County, ambled the subject of this story, young Archie Wainwright, who came to be known as the Scourge of Stagecoach Road and who, for a short period of time in 1976, the summer of his eighteenth year, terrorized his little portion of Brome County.

Archie was born in 1958 on the Wainwright farm located on Stagecoach Road, near the intersection of Mount Echo Road. The farm is no longer there however, the Wainwrights having sold the property in 1978 to some rich Montrealers who tore down the farmhouse and old outbuildings and erected an equestrian estate the likes of which would rival anything on Knowlton's Lakeside Road, or anywhere else in Brome County for that matter. The Wainwrights left Brome County and moved to Nova Scotia where they had family. It was commonly accepted that they left due to the shame and dishonor that Archie's activities had brought to the family name.

Archie Wainwright was the fourth of six kids born there on the farm. And there was nothing on the home front to suggest why he had gone bad. He had a good and devoted mother, Irene; a hard-working father, Henry and normal siblings. Some people were of the opinion that the large red birthmark that covered the right side of Archie's face might have contributed to his foul temperament. It was the shape of an apple with a stem still in it. Those same people reported stories of Archie, as a young child, being mercilessly teased by the other kids during his time at Knowlton Academy. John Craft of Brome Village believed it had nothing to do with the birthmark. Craft was adamant: Archie Wainwright was just a bad seed. A very bad seed.

As a youngster, Archie was suspended so often from Knowlton Academy for fighting with his fellow students that his mother finally decided to homeschool him. Growing up, his transgressions were relatively minor, but when he hit puberty, he became a public nuisance. By eighteen, he was a full-blown terror.

In his early teens, he had gotten around on bicycle but when he turned eighteen, he began driving. He didn't have his own vehicle so he would borrow his father's pickup or his brother Billy's dirt bike. Without permission, of course. They would not report their vehicle stolen to the police because, well, that just wasn't done.

After a half-dozen or so such incidents, brother Billy, who had told Archie many times to never again take his bike without permission, waited for Archie to return home. When he did, Billy, who outweighed Archie by thirty pounds, dragged him into the barn and gave him a proper thrashing.

Henry Wainwright also objected to Archie taking his pickup but stopped short of taking Archie to the barn for a beating. But Henry did hide the keys. Archie, however, was nothing if not resourceful, and soon learned how to hotwire his dad's pickup. It was not that difficult in those days. Today, I am told, cars are impossible to hotwire.

When Henry saw that Archie had learned how to hotwire the truck, he decided on a new tactic. He disconnected the distributor cap from the coil thereby rendering the vehicle unstartable, undriveable. But Archie soon figured it out. He opened the hood and seeing the disconnected wire, simply re-connected it and he was on his way.

The elder Wainwright then went into his workshop in the garage and found among his used parts a defective connector wire which for some unknown reason, he had never thrown out. He took the defective wire and used it to connect the coil to the distributor cap. He tested it. The truck would not start.

The next time Archie went out to the barn to borrow his dad's truck, it would not start. He popped the hood, searched high and low for a cause but could not resolve the issue. This whole game of mechanical cat-and-mouse between Archie and his dad would have seemed almost comedic had it not been so intrinsically sad. Archie felt there was only one option left to him.

He walked along Stagecoach Road all the way to Mount Echo Road, turned right and walked to East Hill. There he stole a pickup truck from the new owners of the old Sullivan farm, people from the city who were there only on weekends.

Eventually, Irene and Henry decided to let Archie have their old '61 Chevy pickup, the one that Henry usually scavenged for spare parts. They told Archie if he could get it running again, he could use it. Archie's parents never intended to reward their son's poor behavior. They just wanted to keep him out of jail for as long as they could. They had no doubt that's where he was headed. Little did they know that Archie would never go to jail. He would never even be arrested. The police would never even get to lay eyes on him.

So, now with his rusty but refurbished '61 Chevy pickup, Archie was mobile. At first, he stuck to Stagecoach Road where the chances of running into the police were relatively slim. Of course, Archie didn't have a driver's license and had no intention of ever getting one.

One of his frequent stops was the Craft General Store in Brome Village right across from the fairgrounds. Archie's father had an account there so Archie would grab smokes and a soft drink or anything else he wanted, including work clothes. Archie told John Craft, the proprietor, to put it on the family tab. Initially, his dad would balk at the charges but would eventually pay them. But one day, Henry Wainwright told John Craft that he would no longer cover Archie's purchases and that Craft would have to deal with Archie on his own. That decision was one that Henry Wainwright came to regret.

John Craft, a large, impressive figure who always dressed in a plaid shirt and denim overalls, a man who very few locals would mess with, accepted the challenge. The next time Archie came in, Craft told him that he would have to pay for the items he took or he, Craft, would report them as thefts to the police.

"You do that, and you'll be sorry," said Archie.

After the third such incident and after refusing to pay his tab, which at that point was over one hundred dollars, John Craft did indeed call the SQ and reported the incidents. That brought patrol officers to the Craft store to take a complaint and, eventually, to the Wainwright farm to question Henry and Irene because as usual, Archie could not be found.

Henry Wainwright was forthcoming about his son being a troubled lad and prone to hooliganism although he was a decent son to both parents. Irene explained that Archie had been named after her brother who was a lost soul as well, in and out of trouble for most of his life. Irene confessed that she'd made a mistake naming her son after her brother. It had hexed the poor boy, she claimed. Henry too expressed his disappointment in Archie's behavior. When asked by the police when Archie would be home, Henry honestly responded that they had no idea. He came and went as he pleased. Archie, they were ashamed to admit, was beyond their control. When the officers asked the Wainwrights if they would call them when Archie was there, they said they would but they never did. The Wainwrights did not condone their son's comportment, but they just couldn't bring themselves to actually turn him in.

Two nights after Archie learned from his parents that John Craft had reported the incidents and that the SQ had come to the house looking for him, two Molotov cocktails were thrown through the front window of the Craft General Store. The building burned to the ground before the Sutton Fire department, who served the town, could get there. When questioned by the SQ about possible suspects for the arson, John Craft was adamant: "I have no doubt in my mind. It was that freak, Archie Wainwright!"

Everyone knew that Archie had done it, and Archie didn't hide it either. In fact, every time he drove through Brome Village and he spotted John Craft rocking on the porch of his house, located next to the ruins of the store, he would slow down and flick a book of unopened matches toward the old man. It was as much an admission of guilt as it was a threat. John Craft did not rebuild or reopen the store. He was done. He was retired.

The investigators, with the assistance of their arson squad from headquarters in Montreal had conducted a thorough investigation of the scene and the fire was deemed to have been intentional, therefore criminal, ergo arson, and Archie Wainwright was named as the prime suspect. When Archie learned that the SQ had visited his parents again and told them that their son was the prime suspect in the arson, Archie visited the Craft residence again, and under cover of darkness, treated the Craft family to two shotgun blasts through the front windows of their home. John Craft never reported that incident. He simply had the windows repaired and decided to let sleeping dogs, or rather rabid dogs, lie.

Jacques Latendresse, who was one of the investigators explained to me that while Wainwright was their prime suspect, they had no concrete evidence linking him to the fire. Jacques often said that what the police know and what they are able to prove are two different matters.

Having caused enough trouble in Brome Village for the time being, Archie ventured west along Stagecoach Road to where it joined Highway 104. Right there, at Gilman's Corner, where the 104 and the 139 intersect, stood the Gilmore Hotel. This is where Archie had his first taste of alcohol, and he took to it like a fish to water. His parents weren't drinkers, so he had never had as much as a beer until he set foot in the Gilmore. And it would come as no surprise to anyone who knew Archie that he was a mean drunk. Sober, he was bad enough but with some beer in him, he took his orneriness to a whole new level.

He began by stopping in for a beer in the afternoon or evening and minding his own business but in no time, he became a one-man wrecking crew. He got into fistfights with other patrons almost every time he went there. But bar owners in those days were more relaxed than today. If someone acted up on Saturday night, they were not necessarily barred from ever returning. Again, it was like the old West in those days. A certain amount of rough-housing was to be expected. And most owners and their doormen were capable of handling all comers.

One afternoon, when Archie was leaving the Gilmore, owner Ernest Lacombe spotted Archie reading a poster on the door, advertising live entertainment the following Saturday night. This was the era of the dancing girls.

Archie returned that Saturday night, and he became totally enthralled with this new form of spectacle. Ernest Lacombe, it turned out, was a visionary. So successful were his Saturday nights, that Lacombe had to turn people away at the door lest the Gilmore exceed its legal capacity.

One fateful Saturday night, while Archie was at the Gilmore, and having had a few beers, he became so smitten by the talent on stage that he clambered up and tried to dance with the young lady. Her name was Gabriella Amor and she was as graceful and supple as a ballerina and was going about proving it to the sounds of "Love Hurts" by Nazareth. As soon as Archie got on stage, two bouncers were up there with him. The crowd jeered and booed at having their frolic trifled with. The startled Gabriella retreated backstage and was peering through the purple velvet curtains as the two bouncers grabbed Archie by his arms and legs and carried him off the stage and to the door leading to the parking lot. The patrons, who did not appreciate Archie's interfering with Gabriella's artistry, applauded Archie's ejection from the Gilmore. He was tossed into the parking lot and blocked from re-entry, so he got into his rattling pickup, gunned the engine, popped the clutch, and sped away, throwing a plume of parking lot gravel and dirt behind him.

But on the final Saturday night that Archie would drink at the Gilmore, two vigilant servers saw Archie arrive and told him he could have one beer and then he'd have to leave. He agreed. But after that one beer, he refused to depart, and when the two servers tried to forcibly escort him to the door, a fight broke out. Archie was quickly overpowered and carried outside, again by his legs and arms. Many of the patrons there that night followed the three men outside. They watched as Archie attempted to fight the two men, and then watched as the two gave Archie a whooping. They didn't break any bones because they were pros and knew better. But they did pummel him pretty bad and then carried him to his pickup and told him to leave and never come back. They assured him that if he ever did, they would send him to the hospital.

The next Friday night, after all patrons had left, the Gilmore Hotel burned to the ground. At the request of the Brome Lake Police who were responsible for West Brome, the SQ conducted the fire investigation and after having spoken with Ernest Lacombe, their prime suspect was Archie Wainwright. But they could not prove anything as there were no witnesses to place Archie at the scene at the time of the fire.

While the era of dancing girls was new to Archie, it was getting a little old in West Brome. The neighboring communities, which included Cowansville were not at all thrilled at having lewd entertainment in the area. And while it was by no means a common occurrence, sometimes wives showed up at the Gilmore to retrieve their errant husbands. On one occasion, an angry spouse, a petite woman with flaming red hair, marched into the Gilmore searching for her missing husband. Finding him sitting at a table with friends, drinking beer and gawking at a young woman on stage, dressed like a schoolgirl, gyrating and slowly unbuttoning her vest, the woman threw a screaming fit, pointed to the door, and shrieked at her husband to leave immediately and go home to his children. The man rose and, thoroughly embarrassed, headed solemnly for the door, with his wife, fists clenched, pacing indignantly behind him, hurling obscenities at him. The other men cheered. Watching a disgruntled wife emasculate her husband in front of strangers proved to be almost as entertaining as the dancing girls. Almost, but not quite.

Ernest Lacombe could see the writing on the wall. He knew that this form of entertainment, while profitable, had a limited future. Its days were numbered. Citizens were putting increasing pressure on town councils to amend their bylaws to outlaw nude dancers within town limits. So, after the fire, Ernest Lacombe collected the insurance money and, instead of rebuilding, decided to take up the rocking chair. The era of the dancing girls came to an end in West Brome. He sold the property and today a lumber yard stands in its place.

With the Gilmore now gone, Archie redirected his patronage to the Prince of Wales Hotel in Abercorn. Knowing his home territory like the back of his hand, Archie knew how to drive the backroads from home to Abercorn with minimum use of numbered highways, thereby pretty much steering clear of police patrol cars.

At the Prince of Wales, Archie enjoyed picking fights with American boys who loved to cross the border to get their drink on. Canadian beer was stronger than American brew and the Prince of Wales closed at 3 a.m. instead of at 1, like the bars did in Vermont. For Archie, an evening out without a fist fight was like a day without sunshine.

Archie's nemesis at the Prince of Wales was a barman called Leon. He was tall, strong and for exercise, lifted logs instead of barbells and flipped used truck tires in the parking lot for the sheer pleasure of it. Also, he was nimble for a big guy; he could handle himself very well. Legend had it that Leon was a veteran of the bars of the mining towns in Northern Quebec and had yet to meet his match. One evening, when Archie started getting rowdy, Leon asked him to leave. Archie refused and Leon escorted him outside. Archie put up a valiant struggle but had his ass handed to him and found himself incapable of driving. At 5 a.m., as Leon was leaving the Prince of Wales, he checked on Archie who was just stirring in the back of his pickup in the parking lot, awakening to the tweets and chirpings of redwing blackbirds. He was bloodied, battered, and bruised. No broken bones, though. Leon was a pro.

The following Thursday night, after closing hours, the Prince of Wales Hotel burned to the ground. Today, Le Parc des Pionniers is located at the site. There is also a tourist marker that celebrates not only the Prince of Wales but numerous other drinking establishments that had thrived during the prohibition era, among them, the notorious *Bucket of Blood.* There is no mention of Archie Wainwright, the Scourge of Stagecoach Road, who was one of the Prince of Wales' most notorious patrons and the one who, according to local legend, razed it to the ground.

With both the Gilmore and Prince of Wales gone, Archie took to traveling all the way to Mansonville for his Saturday night mischief. Again, being a consummate back roads-man, he could make the trek between home and Mansonville by using mostly dirt roads, such as Stagecoach and Baker Talc or maybe Mountain Road in South Bolton, thereby eluding any cops who, for the most part, stuck to the major highways and were otherwise preoccupied with the summer Olympics.

Ah yes, the summer Olympics. A word about that might help to put things into some perspective. In 1976, the year in which this story takes place, the summer during which Archie's activities peaked, was the same year that Montreal hosted the summer Olympics. What did this have to do with Brome County? Well, all equestrian events were held in Bromont, and while Bromont was not in Brome County, it was close enough to involve the Cowansville detachment. Also, 1976 was just four years after the 1972 Olympics which were held in Munich. During that event, one may recall, Palestinian terrorists stormed the athletes' village and killed eleven Israelis. So, understandably, Canadian authorities were on high alert and were taking every measure to prevent any act of terrorism or sabotage. And if that were not enough pressure for the SQ, Princess Anne, the only daughter of Queen Elizabeth, as a member of the British Olympic team, was competing in the three-day horse event. As Jacques Latendresse clearly explained the situation to me at the time: Most Quebecois couldn't care less if Princess Anne or any other member of the Royal family lived or died. But nothing had better happen in Bromont. Not on their watch.

As a result, regular SQ patrols in its habitual territory were scaled back. Some officers were seconded to Bromont for the duration of the games. The officers who remained were on twelve-hour shifts in the months prior to and during the games, and were instructed to check with clockwork regularity, a predetermined list of potential targets, for example, all Hydro Quebec stations and substations, Bell Canada stations, radio towers and antennae, hospitals, and so on. It goes without saying that the likes of Archie Wainwright were not a high priority during that time.

To no one's surprise, Archie's visits to the Mansonville Hotel began, unfolded, and ended much the same way they had in his previous drinking spots. Archie was not about to change his genetic makeup or his behavior. And neither were the hotel owners and patrons of Brome County about to bend over to accommodate the violent tendencies of the Scourge of Stagecoach Road.

On his second-to-last weekend at the Mansonville hotel, after having gotten into a dust up with two fellows from North Troy, Vermont, the owner, Pierre Marchand, ordered Archie to leave. When Archie refused, Marchand, who was alone that night and thought himself capable of handling any of his belligerent patrons, grabbed Archie by the collar and walked him toward the exit. Archie feigned compliance but when they reached the doorway, he swung back with an elbow, and, catching Marchand off guard, broke and bloodied his nose. Archie, seeing Marchand with his open hand under his nose gathering blood, made a quick retreat to his pickup and fled the scene.

For a short period of time in his early days, Pierre Marchand had been a professional wrestler. In fact, he still had friends in the field. He himself was feeling his age but wanted to get his message across to Archie. He called in a favor from one of his former colleagues,

Hugh "The Hammer" Gendron of Montreal, so he invited Gendron to come out for the weekend.

When Archie arrived on Saturday night, Marchand told him he was not welcome. Archie responded with "Fuck You" and "Get me a beer." Marchand went behind the bar and knocked on a door at the end of the counter and "The Hammer," all 6 foot 5, and 275 lbs. of him, emerged. He approached Archie's table and told him to leave. Archie once again pretended to obey as The Hammer walked him toward the door. But suddenly, Archie picked up an empty chair. He swung around and aimed it at The Hammer's head. The Hammer was expecting something of the sort. He caught the chair in his hand. He gently placed it on the floor. He then shot a left jab at Archie's solar plexus. Archie went flying into a wall. An ancient set of deer antlers fell from high on the wall in a cloud of dust, narrowly missing Archie, nearly impaling him. Gendron picked Archie up by the hair. He stood him up then punched him, hard, in the front of the left shoulder. The impact looked like it dislocated Archie's shoulder. He fell to his knees. Archie raised his good arm in mock surrender and got up. But while still facing The Hammer, Archie took a chance and threw Gendron a kick to the groin. The Hammer was expecting as much and caught Archie's leg mid-air. He held onto the foot and swung Archie around three times much to the amusement of the other patrons. The dozen or so drinkers cheered as the Hammer then dragged Archie by the leg, out the door, through the gravel parking lot to Archie's pickup. The Hammer looked back toward Marchand who was standing in the doorway, surrounded by the other customers who were watching the spectacle. Marchand nodded that

that was indeed Archie's pickup. The Hammer picked Archie up by the legs and the neck, twirled him around over his head several times—a signature move The Hammer called the Tilt-a-Whirl—and threw Archie into the bed of his truck. He landed with a loud metallic thud. The Hammer pointed a finger at Archie and said, "Never come back here."

Archie managed to get into his pickup and drive away despite his injured shoulder. Four days later, in the middle of the night, the Mansonville Hotel went up in flames. Today, located diagonally opposite the Town Hall, a lovely parking lot adorns the site. No plaque, though. No sign. No mention of the numerous fights and brawls that had occurred there and especially no mention of the final match between Hugh "The Hammer" Gendron and Archie Wainwright, the Scourge of Stagecoach Road.

Curiously though, in spite of Archie's predilection for over-drinking and violent flare-ups, there was one establishment where Archie never caused any trouble. Why would he? At the Thirsty Boot, he was greeted like family. Sort of like Norm on the TV show *Cheers*. Located just outside of Knowlton, on the Bolton Pass Road, locals would offer to buy him a beer. He would play cards with his fellow patrons, talk about car engines and dirt bikes, or about the roads least likely to be patrolled by the SQ. The Thirsty Boot was his refuge, his home away from home. To this day, the Thirsty Boot still stands where it always has. It has changed owners several times and has been closed for periods of time, but the Thirsty Boot never succumbed to fire.

Annette and Amberson Toomey lived on Stagecoach Road right in Brome Village, within walking distance to the former Craft General Store and right next to the Brome fairgrounds. The Toomeys were a good, hard-working family. Annette taught school at the Knowlton Academy and Amberson was a long-haul truck driver, often gone to the US for days at a time. It was a happy home. They had one son, Collin, and on his sixteenth birthday, Annette and Amberson bought their son a second-hand dirt bike. Collin loved his bike and parked in the front yard for all to see.

In early June, only a few weeks after having acquired the new dirt bike for her son, Annette was up in the pre-dawn hours, drinking coffee and getting ready for school. She did not sleep well when Amberson was on the road. She heard a noise and looked out the living room window and saw Archie Wainwright, with a pickup truck and a ramp, and she watched incredulously as the bastard tried to push Collin's bike up the ramp and into the bed of his pickup. She yelled upstairs for Collin and ran outside in her nightgown. As she ran toward him, Archie lay the bike on its side and picked up a tire iron from the bed of his truck and lifted his arm, which Annette took as a serious threat. She stopped dead in her tracks. Archie sneered. Now, Collin came running out of the house in just his pajama bottoms and when he neared Archie, he was greeted with three strong whacks of the tire iron to his rib cage. Collin fell to the ground, his mother grabbing him into her arms, shielding her son from further blows. Archie laughed. And, because stealth was no longer crucial, Archie hotwired the bike, while mother and son cowered in the grass, cranked it up and drove it up the ramp, into the bed of his pickup. He lay it down, jumped to the ground and placed the ramp in the bed of the truck. He got into the cab and started up his pickup. As he turned out of their driveway, he honked his horn and waved an arm out the window to Annette and Collin.

"You fucking freak!" yelled Collin as Archie drove off.

Annette, still holding her son, shushed him and said quietly, "Honey, don't call him that."

Annette and Collin made their way back into the house. Annette called Amberson on her CB radio. Amberson was snoozing at a rest stop on the I-95 in northern North Carolina at the time. Amberson told Annette to call the SQ immediately and report the incident, which she did. The SQ came to the house and took a report. They dropped by again the next day to tell Annette that they had gone to the Wainwright farm twice the day before but could not find Archie or any sign of Collin's bike. They said they would keep looking and that the detachment investigators were also on the case.

Two days later, two SQ investigators visited the Wainwrights looking for Archie. Jacques Latendresse was one of the two. Archie was nowhere to be found and his parents did not know where he was.

The next night at 3 AM, while Amberson was at the Lacolle border crossing, waiting for his truck to be inspected, Annette heard a loud crash downstairs, coming from the living room. She looked out the bedroom window and saw the taillights of a pickup truck speed away. She hurried downstairs and saw a bottle on fire on the living room floor. It was a Molotov Cocktail and it had crashed through the living room window. But somehow, miraculously, it had not shattered and had not ignited. It lay there with a piece of cloth stuffed into its neck, burning. Not knowing exactly what to do, instinctively and courageously, Annette picked up the incendiary device and flung it back through the broken window. It crashed on a rock in the flower garden on the front lawn, exploded into flames and burned itself out.

Annette called Amberson and then the SQ and reported this new incident. Later that day, Amberson arrived home to a distraught wife and son. He consoled them and told them everything would be okay.

Later, after dinner, Amberson drove to the Wainwright farm and was there for about fifteen minutes. He came home close to seven-thirty.

Archie Wainwright stole, fought, set fires and generally wreaked havoc up and down Stagecoach Road and in Brome County for just one summer, the summer of his eighteenth year, the summer of the '76 Olympics. And just like that, it all came to a sudden halt. It all stopped. No one ever heard from Archie Wainwright again. That was it. He was gone. No one knew where. It was a mystery,

I can't say exactly what happened to Archie Wainwright but I can confirm that no one I knew in Brome County ever heard from him again. He was gone and presumed by many to be dead, having finally pushed his luck too far with someone who *did* break bones, and who was not inclined to leave him whole.

In late August, after the Olympics were over, the SQ went to see the Wainwright family at their farm. Jacques Latendresse told me that they still had Archie Wainwright as prime suspect for a number of offenses and asked old man Wainwright if he had any idea of Archie's whereabouts. The two SQ investigators stood in the kitchen talking to Mr. Wainwright while Mrs. Wainwright sat in a chair at the kitchen table just watching them talk. Jacques said she had a sadness about her that was heartbreaking. She said nothing, preferring instead to let her husband talk to the officers. The old man said that he hadn't seen or heard from Archie in weeks.

"Actually," said Henry, looking at his wife and then back at the officers. "We have no proof of it, but we think our son is dead."

"Why do you think that?" Jacques asked.

"Because it's been just too long. He's never been away from us this long."

"Do you think he was in an accident?" asked Jacques.

The old man again turned to his wife and then back to the two investigators.

"We're pretty sure someone killed him." The old man wiped his brow with a hanky. "But we have no idea who it could be. We have no information. As you know, Archie had many enemies."

The two investigators left their business cards with Mr. Wainwright who examined the cards and placed them in a sugar bowl on the kitchen counter which seemed to contain dozens of such cards.

"Please let us know if you hear anything," Latendresse said.

"We will." The old man said it in a way that said they wouldn't.

The investigators left and never returned.

But they did see the Toomeys again given that the assault on Collin, the theft of the dirt bike and the incident with the Molotov cocktail were the last incidents on record involving Archie Wainwright.

Amberson Toomey explained that after Archie had tried to firebomb his house, Amberson went to see Mr. Wainwright and asked him to give Archie a message: Come meet me at the far end of the fairgrounds the following evening at 9 p.m.

Amberson explained that Mr. Wainwright, upon hearing the story of what Archie had done to Annette and Collin, expressed great sadness and sympathy, and promised that if he saw Archie, he would give him the message.

"The next evening," said Amberson, "I went to the fairgrounds, but Archie never showed up. I waited a long time, way past 10 p.m.

Latendresse asked, "What did you plan to do with Archie if he showed up."

"I would probably have given him the thrashing of his life." He hesitated. "But he never showed up. I think he knew what was waiting for him."

Over the years, from my contacts in Brome County and Brome Village, I heard many theories about what might have happened to Archie. They ranged from whimsical to wishful thinking: Archie had joined the Canadian Armed Forces and was now stationed in

Germany; Archie had crossed the border into the US, had joined the Marines and had died in Vietnam; Archie had joined the carnival circuit and was now forever on the move across Canada. Someone else said that they were certain they had seen Archie at an agricultural fair in Brooklin, Ontario in 1980 where he was manning the controls of the Ferris Wheel. That same person said that he thought he recognized Archie because of the birthmark on his right cheek. Another rumor had Archie having joined a religious cult that was popular in northern Alberta. The theories went on and on. One thing was certain: Archie Wainwright was gone from Brome County. His reign of terror was over.

Part III
The Ethics Committee

In August, 2024, almost fifty years after Archie disappeared, the saddest thing happened. My friend and long-time drinking companion, Jacques Latendresse passed away. The funeral announcement did not include any details about the cause of death except for saying that he died following a lengthy illness. I presumed that the illness was alcoholism or something alcohol-related. I quit drinking in 2000, as a new millennium resolution, but Jacques did not stop. He told me he had no intention of ever stopping. He enjoyed it too much. He retired in 2003 and we slowly lost contact after that.

Anyways, the funeral was held in Cowansville, at the Despatie Funeral Home. Of course, I attended even though I have never liked funerals. Even funerals for people who are not close to me. The finality of life gets to me. I swear, inside, I feel like I'm on the verge of tears. Oh, I control it, no worries, but it gets to me. Then I see people huddled in small groups, talking, smiling, sometimes laughing, and I don't get it. Shouldn't a funeral be somber? I remember even as a teenager, at my Uncle Harry's funeral, my very first, I wanted to shout out: *What's wrong with you people? This is not a party. This is not a family reunion. Talk quietly, solemnly.* I don't know. Maybe it's just me.

The place was packed and a good number of the people in attendance, I think, were cops, but it was difficult to be sure. Cops today often look like their civilian counterparts, some even sporting close-cropped beards. Back in the 1970s and 80s, you could tell right away. The short hair and mustaches. That look was ubiquitous. But today it's different. They blend in better.

As I entered the main salon, I saw the closed casket and was instantly relieved that I would not have to look at a cadaver. I didn't want to see Jacques that way. Open caskets are grotesque. I despise them. I never approach them.

On the casket was a framed photograph of Jacques from his younger years as a patrol officer. In the photo, he was smiling. What a smile. I knew it well. Near the casket I could see his family, standing, in a kind of row. His widow, Denise, was there, and his two sons, Marc and Michel, and the youngest, his daughter Hélène, all grown up now. I hadn't seen them in such a long time.

There was a short line of people waiting to offer their sympathies and so I joined the queue. When it was my turn, I advanced and offered them my most sincere condolences. In French, of course. I can speak and write French decently although, even after all these years, I can still trip up the masculine and the feminine of certain nouns, the *le* and the *la*.

The family looked at me and softly said, *Merci*. I told them that I had known Jacques for many years while I was a reporter and that we had been good friends.

Marc, the eldest son, perked up and asked if I was the guy who his dad used to drink with at the Yamaska.

I said, "Oui, c'est moi. Je suis Alistair Mackenzie."

The daughter, Hélène, smiled and said that her father often spoke of me. "Vous êtes alors Aliss?" she asked.

I smiled. "Oui, je suis Aliss." Jacques liked to tease me by calling me *Aliss* instead of *Alistair*. He would often toast me: "I drink to you, Aliss!" I would tease him back by saying, "And I drink to you, monsieur Tenderness."

I smiled and again offered my condolences and just before turning away and leaving the family to other visitors waiting in line, I said, "Il était mon ami. Un bon ami."

They smiled and nodded. Denise had a handkerchief in her right hand. She dabbed her right eye. I slowly moved away, leaving room for others to approach the family.

I saw a large-screen TV on a distant wall which I presumed was playing a slideshow of Jacques at various stages of his life. I walked over and watched the loop for a while. It was nice to see Jacques in such a healthy environment, with family and friends on camping adventures, on boating excursions, on Christmas mornings, and at family gatherings, his children always smiling. The only images I had of Jacques and myself were in my mind and were of us at the Yamaska or some other dingy bar in Brome County. Not much of a slide show potential there. I also noticed that in almost every photo, Jacques had a beer in his hand. But I was happy to add these photos to my mind's memory of Jacques even though I was not in any of them.

I saw a young man standing by himself near a large window that overlooked the Yamaska River which coursed its way through the town of Cowansville. I didn't necessarily want to talk to him or anyone else, but I didn't want to stand alone, like a lost soul, so I moved in his general direction. Also, he looked Anglophone. Don't ask me how I knew. I just did. Anglos are very adept at spotting their compatriots in a crowd of Francophones.

Now, standing closer to the young man, I nodded in his direction and turned to look over the people, about one hundred strong. The only person I recognized was François Babouin whom I knew from the old days but not that well. Babouin was older than the others and had to be closing in on retirement at this point. He was standing with a female cop, late 20s, maybe early 30s. I didn't recognize any others. For sure in the 70s I would have because I spent a lot of time at the courthouse, following cases and watching the police testify. That was my job. I had known all of them. But not today. I have been out of the business too long.

After a few minutes, I turned to the young man next to me.

"Nice service."

"Yes," he responded.

"Hi, I'm Alistair."

He put out his hand, so I shook it. It's always a tentative thing, nowadays, isn't it? Shaking hands? Since COVID, that is. Not everyone wants to do it. It's like you need their permission to shake hands.

"Hi. I'm Finn," he said.

"Finn?" I repeated.

"Yes, Finnian Toomey. But call me Finn."

"Ah," I said. "I was at your christening."

"What?"

"I knew your dad, Collin."

"Really?"

"And your grandparents, Amberson and Annette."

"Oh," he said, "you must be that reporter."

"Yes, Alistair Mackenzie. *Retired* reporter."

"Well, isn't that something," he said. He shook his head a little then asked, "I guess you knew Mr. Latendresse from your days as a reporter?"

"I knew him better than that," I said. "He was a good friend. We used to hang out a lot. In our younger days especially."

"Oh, nice."

"Yes," I said, "but may I ask how you knew him?"

"Oh yeah," Finn said, "I didn't have a lot of contact with him but one night, when I was leaving the Thirsty Boot, he pulled up next to me in the parking lot. He rolled down his window and asked me if I was Finn Toomey. I said I was. He said that there were several roadblocks that night, one of them at Owen's Corner. Police were checking for impaired drivers. He suggested I leave my pickup there, at the Boot, and let him drive me home to Brome Village."

"Really?" I said.

"Yeah, so, he drove me home. He was an investigator at this time, and he had an unmarked car. And he was right: There *was* a checkpoint at Owen's Corner, intersection of 215 and 104. Anyway, they *were* checking for drunk drivers. They waved Mr. Latendresse through, and he drove me home. I really appreciated that. I thought that was very thoughtful of him."

"It was," I said. "Why do you think he did that?"

"I asked him that very thing and he said he knew my grandparents and felt bad that they never caught the guy who threatened my grandma and beat up my dad. There was this guy. He stole Dad's dirt bike and beat him with a tire iron. That was back in the 70s. 1976, I think. I told him that was okay. It was all in the past and I was sure that the guy got what he deserved."

"That was Archie Wainwright," I said. "The guy who did that."

"Yes," said Finn. "Good memory. Archie Wainwright."

"Well, that was nice of him," I said. "I mean Jacques. For driving you."

"Yes, it was. No one had ever done something like that for me. Not a cop, anyway. I never forgot it. So, when I heard that he had passed away, I thought I'd come by and pay my respects."

"Well, he was a good man. It was nice of you to come today."

"You know," said Finn, "they never found Archie Wainwright but they did find my dad's dirt bike. Did you know that?"

"They did? I did not know that."

"Yes, when the Wainwrights sold their farm, the new owners took down all the buildings, and when they were leveling out the land, a dozer happened upon the dirt bike cached in a mound of dirt and manure, out behind the barn."

"Wow, amazing."

Just then, from the corner of my eye, I saw the female cop I had noticed earlier, approaching us. She stopped in front of Finn.

"Hi Finn," she said. "Thanks for coming today. That was thoughtful of you."

Finn nodded, smiled and said, "Sorry to hear about Mr. Latendresse."

"Thank you," she said and asked, "How are you doing?"

"I'm fine," said Finn, "and you?"

"I'm doing well," she said, smiling softly. She looked at Finn a little too long, I thought.

Then she turned toward me. "Are you Mr. Mackenzie?" she asked.

I was taken aback. I sure was popular today.

"Yes, I am," I said.

"I'm Jojo Alison," she said. "Jacques always talked about you, how you were good friends going way back."

Ah, so this was Jojo Alison, I thought. Jacques had mentioned her several times. A very competent police officer with a promising future, he had said. I was finally putting a face to the name.

"Thank you," I said "Yes, Jacques and I were good friends. Especially in the old days."

"You two used to hang out at the Yam, didn't you?"

"Yes, we did," I said smiling. "The Yamaska was our hideout."

"Well, thank you for being his friend," she said. "Any friend of Jacques is a friend of mine."

She put her hand out. We shook. She had a firm handshake and a certain confidence about her. She was charming but not phony.

"I'd better get back," she said, motioning with her head to the group of cops she had been standing with.

She looked at Finn and said, "You take care, Finn."

"Yes, I will," he said.

She turned and began walking away. After a few steps, Finn blurted out, "Thank . . . thank you. And . . . and you too."

She turned, smiled a warm smile, only at him, not me, then turned and left.

Okay, I am no longer a reporter, but I still fancy myself a decent observer of the human experience. I have an eye for things, and there was something going on there between Jojo and Finn. There was a history there. Dare I say, chemistry? They were both in the same age bracket, both extremely good-looking, both tall with dirty blond hair. I could see them together. So I had to dig deeper.

"Nice lady," I said.

"Oh, yeah," he said.

"Anything there between you two?"

"Oh, no," said Finn. "Only in my dreams. Not that I didn't try. But she was nice enough to let me down easy. Better that way, I guess. We come from two different worlds."

"I understand," I said.

"But she's super nice," Finn said. He sounded like a kid. Hell, he was a kid.

"How did you two meet? I asked. "Oops, maybe I shouldn't ask that."

"Yeah, well, exactly. She once busted me for possession. A little weed. But it never went anywhere. That was in 2018."

"Oh good," I said. "It's all legal now anyhow, right? I think that was the year it was decriminalized."

"Well, for certain quantities, it was," he said. "But she is a good person. I had a big crush on her." He smiled. "I guess it doesn't happen often that a guy has a crush on his arresting officer."

I laughed. "For sure," I said. "But I completely understand. She is a charmer."

"Oh, yes, most definitely," he said.

I looked around the reception area one more time.

"Well," I said, "I've paid my respects, and I don't know anyone else here. I think I'll take my leave if you don't mind."

"I was thinking the same thing, Mr. Mackenzie. Mind if I walk out with you?"

"Sure," I said. "My pleasure." We turned and headed for the main doorway.

Outside in the parking lot, I turned to Finn and said, "You know all the cops felt very bad at the time—Jacques told me this—that they never caught Archie Wainwright for what he did to your grandmother and your dad. And to the other people he had victimized in Brome Village. And the fires, the destruction. But he just disappeared. I felt bad too because I knew your grandparents. I even met your dad, Collin. He was a kid at the time. Anyways, it was a shame that Archie was never brought to justice."

"I think we all get what we deserve in the end," said Finn. "Don't you?"

"I'm not so sure about that," I said.

"Do you know what Archie's nickname was in school?" asked Finn.

"In school?" I asked.

"Well, before he was thrown out in the sixth grade."

I shook my head.

"The Freak," he said. "They called him The Freak. Because of the red blotch on his face."

"The Freak?" I repeated.

"Yep, but not to his face. Because he'd come after you. And if he heard you'd said it behind his back, he'd come after you even harder

"I didn't know that."

"Yeah, my dad told me that," said Finn. "Did you know that my dad went to school with Archie?"

"No, but I guess it makes sense. They were sort of the same age, weren't they?"

"Yep," said Finn. "My dad was three years younger. He knew Archie but because of the age difference, he didn't have much to do with him. But Dad saw it all. How the kids called him The Freak. My dad said Archie was not a bully back then. He didn't pick on kids. But if you called him The Freak, he'd get you. Even older or bigger kids. He wasn't afraid of anyone. He'd just go after them."

"I never heard that part of the story," I said. "But still, I wonder what happened to him. I mean in 1976. One minute he was there, and the next, he was gone."

"There were plenty of rumors," said Finn.

"Oh yeah," I said, "plenty of rumors. In the years following, there were more sightings of Archie Wainwright than there were of Elvis Presley."

Finn laughed.

"One rumor," I said, "had him joining the Marines and dying in Vietnam but that war was over in '75 so that wasn't possible."

"People can change," said Finn. "But yeah, I heard all those stories."

Finn hesitated for a moment, looked around then looked back at me. "Did you hear any rumors about the committee?"

"Committee? What committee?"

Other people were now emerging from the funeral home and began milling about, a few lighting up cigarettes. We were no longer alone. Finn nodded in the direction of a small grassy area in the middle of the parking lot, a tiny oasis with a large elm tree and a picnic bench where I presumed employees might eat lunch and escape the odor of formaldehyde. We walked in that direction.

"Yeah, the committee," said Finn. "According to some, Brome Village had this committee. Some called it the Ethics Committee."

Oh, oh, I thought. I hoped Finn was not going to try and drag me into some conspiracy theory. "Where did you hear that from, Finn?"

"Hey Mr. Mackenzie, are you asking me to reveal my sources?"

"Touché, Finn. Sorry about that. Occupational hazard."

Finn smiled. "Yeah, so the rumor was that this committee would take it upon itself to deal with undesirable behavior in the village: really scary speeders, wife beaters, public drunkards who just wouldn't clean up their act, things like that. They would confront the offenders and explain to them that they couldn't be doing things like that in Brome Village. Sometimes, if they had to, they would hint at unpleasant consequences if things continued. Sometimes, they told the person involved to simply leave town. Permanently."

"You mean by sundown?" I asked.

"Yeah, sort of like that," said Finn. "I heard that the committee would have dealt with Archie earlier, but Archie didn't live in the village. But when he beat up my dad, they made an exception. No one saw anything, but what some people think is that Archie was brought to the fairgrounds and given an ultimatum: leave town or else. Given Archie's reputation, some doubted that he would have left quietly, on his own. The same people said that a fight probably broke out and Archie was killed right then and there, and buried in the swampland off that path, the old railroad track that leads from the fairgrounds to Moffat Road in Knowlton."

"Are you serious, Finn?"

"Oh, I'm dead serious," he said, "that's what I heard. More than once. But I don't believe a word of it."

"You don't?"

"Nope. I think Archie left town and maybe settled down somewhere else, for a fresh start. Maybe to mend his ways."

"Jesus," I said. I wasn't sure what to believe. Did Brome Village really have a vigilante committee? Is that what Finn was suggesting? Did Finn really believe that Archie had relocated? Or had Archie been "relocated" to the wetlands behind the fairgrounds? I really wasn't sure what I believed or what I wanted to believe.

"Anyway," he said. "Those were different times, weren't they, Mr. Mackenzie. You were around in those days. You wouldn't believe a story like that, would you? That the committee took him out back and killed him?"

"Of course, not," I said, but secretly I wasn't so sure.

"Do you believe the story about the committee?" he asked. "That there was such a group?"

"Honestly, Finn, I don't know what to believe. This is all new to me."

"Well, I can tell you that there *was* such a committee," he said.

"You know that for a fact?"

"Yes, I do because I met them. Face to face."

"You did?"

"Yep. They put me on the straight and narrow."

"How do you mean?"

"Well, I told you that Jojo Alison busted me for possession of weed?"

"Yes," I said. But then I put up a finger. "Hold on, Finn. You said you were arrested in 2018. The Archie Wainwright thing was in 1976. That's like, what, over thirty, no, forty years difference."

"Yes, Mr. Mackenzie. Same committee. Different people. That committee has been around for a long, long time. People get old and die. New members come aboard. The committee stays."

Finn considered me for a moment, and I wondered how skeptical my expression was. In truth, I didn't know what I thought. He said, "May I continue?"

"Yes, Finn," I said. "Sorry, please do."

"Anyways, in reality, I was dealing in much larger quantities than what I was arrested for. Quantities that were not legal."

"No!"

"Yep. And the committee didn't want me dealing drugs in Brome Village. Legal or illegal."

"Did they threaten you? This committee?"

"Nope. Not at all. Didn't have to. I was young and stupid and hadn't realized that I might bring shame to the town. I could have moved away from the village, to Cowansville, for example, and continued dealing but I have never lived anywhere else and couldn't see myself anywhere but in Brome Village. It's my home. Can you understand that?"

"Oh, absolutely. I do. For sure."

"So I gave it all up. I stopped dealing and went to trade school instead. I became a heavy equipment operator. That's what I do now. I'm totally legit. And I make a good living."

"Wow."

"Also," Finn added, "I gotta say too that I saw other guys around me who dealt drugs and a few ended up dead. Ever hear of Stubs Lacroix?"

"Oh yes," I said. "Wayne Lacroix. They called him Stubs. He was a musician. A drummer, I think."

"Yep," said Finn. "But he was also a dealer. He ended up dead. They found his body on Tuer road, off Bolton Pass Road. Two in the brain pan." Finn pointed to the back of his head. "Execution style."

"Yes," I said. "I read about it. Not that long ago."

"I bet you don't know this," said Finn as he moved in closer, "I was a suspect in Stub's murder."

"What?" I said.

"Long story short, it wasn't me. I didn't do it. And I had an alibi, but that wasn't enough for the homicide investigators. So they offered me a lie detector test."

"Polygraph," I said.

"Yeah, and I passed. I was exonerated. And they eventually found the killer. A guy from Magog. Stubs wasn't his first. And he didn't even ditch the gun. Police found it in his apartment when they arrested him. Ballistics matched. He was done. Got a life sentence."

"I remember reading about that," I said.

"Yeah," Finn said. "I knew him. Stubs. I had dealings with him." Finn hesitated. "Stubs had a reputation for being a snitch. He was not trustworthy. He even crossed me once. Bad. I was really pissed at him. But I came to my senses before I did anything stupid. Anyway, I sort of expected that it was all going to catch up to him one day. And it did."

"I see."

"Anyway, it's a ruthless business, Mr. Mackenzie. Always has been. And I wanted out. I had to get out. So, I quit. I went straight."

"Well, I'm glad you did," I said.

"I saw the light," Finn said. "And the committee helped me see the light. It changed my life. The question is, did Archie see the light?"

"You're right," I said. "That is the question."

"All we know," said Finn, "is that Brome Village went back to being the quiet little town it always wanted to be. According to my dad, that is. I wasn't there. Wasn't even born yet."

"Well, I was there," I said. "And it's true."

Finn looked around the parking lot, like he was trying to recall where he had parked and then he turned back to me.

"It was nice talking to you," Mr. Mackenzie. "I have to go now. Take care of yourself."

"Thank you, Finn. You take care too." I stood there and watched as he walked to his pickup truck, got in and drove away.

Okay, I thought to myself. I needed time to digest all of this.

Part IV
Reckless Times

There is a tendency among people my age—I am pushing 80—to look back on their younger days with great fondness and nostalgia. The food was tastier back then; the cars we drove, sturdier; the people, nicer; our values, superior. Everything was better. Well, I don't feel that way. I do not think the old days were all that great. I think today is far better than yesterday. I can't speak for the world stage, but here, in Brome County, I think life is pretty good. Better than it was in the 1970s in most respects. Sure, we all have fond memories of our younger years because of our experiences with family and friends. And I do too. But as an era, today outshines the 70s by a long shot.

For example, there is no smoking in restaurants and public places today. That alone should settle any argument. It's amazing how our species, or rather our society, evolved within just one or two generations. The smoking. I doubt that in a hundred years smoking will still exist.

Cars are much safer now, what with multiple airbags, proper seat belts, and automatic braking systems. Satellites in the sky guide you to your destination. How amazing is that? When was the last time you got lost or used a road map? Do they still sell roadmaps?

Today, people follow the rules of the road a lot better than they did back in the day. There are way fewer idiots on the road today. There are still some, for sure, but you get my point. There is far less impaired driving today than back then. And the number of hooligans or crazies who frequent the bars is close to zero these days. No one would tolerate that kind of behavior today. And, of course, today, there are way fewer drinking establishments in Brome County.

The fines for traffic violations in the old days were laughable although we did not realize it at the time. Today the cost is much heavier. Have you gotten a ticket recently? You almost have to take out a loan to pay for it. Plus the demerit points. And this has influenced how we drive. Today, we live in the era of designated drivers. Convictions for impaired driving can result in hefty fines, license suspension and even jail time under the right circumstances. But people in the 70s didn't worry about that. I will be honest here. On occasion, I also drove home while slightly under the influence. I shouldn't have and I'm not proud of it and I would never do it today.

Those were days of recklessness and foolishness. I was part of that era.

I once almost wrote about a crash that occurred in Abercorn. This was in late 1979. At about 3 a.m. on a Sunday morning, two cars collided at the four-way stop at the intersection of Des Eglises and Thibault, killing the four occupants. Apparently, the two boys had started their race when they left Sutton but split up at the entrance of Abercorn. One boy turned left, onto Thibault and raced toward the stop sign at Des Eglises, just under a kilometer away. The other boy sped along the 139 south and turned left at Des Eglises and raced toward the same intersection. Neither boy slowed down upon reaching the stop sign for fear of losing the race. Apparently, their intention was to simply barrel through the intersection and claim victory. Sadly, they both arrived at the precise same moment and the one on Thibault crashed into the other without even braking. They collided with such force that all four occupants were killed instantly with one young woman being ejected through the windshield. None wore a seatbelt. When the police arrived, they thought that only three people had been killed until they found the body of the second girl some forty-five yards away, a crumpled, bloody mess at the foot of a tree.

The boys were both nineteen and the girls, seventeen. The boys were, of course, driving. But what the police didn't understand was that neither boy was driving his own car. They had swapped. When the SQ notified the parents, they learned that the boys, both from Sutton, had a habit of switching autos and racing to a predetermined spot, via different routes, attempting to prove their theory that it was never the car that won a race, it was the driver. This was not their first such race. They often boasted about such exploits to their friends and family.

I was intrigued by the story and decided to do a follow-up. I met with one set of parents and never met with the second. While I was interviewing the parents, I detected a kind of pride in their eyes, almost boastfulness that their son had been a little on the wild side. I didn't see the sadness I had been expecting to see. Were they trying to remember him with fondness or did they really admire his recklessness? Anyway, I couldn't reconcile it within myself. How could parents feel admiration for such wanton behavior? I tried to tell myself that people grieve in different ways, but I couldn't get my head around this.

When I left that night, I abandoned the story. In my mind, the story was no longer about the poor children who had died. It was more about how some people celebrated or admired other people's risky behavior. And I didn't want to write that story. It was too disturbing. I told my editor about it and he agreed that I should kill the story. The theme was something that our readership would not have embraced.

Another time, I was at a dinner party and a woman there told the story of her brother who also had a wild side and who, one evening, while driving too fast with his new Mustang, crashed into a utility pole and ended up a paraplegic. She proceeded to explain that he had just recently taken possession of a new customized Dodge

Challenger, fully equipped with hand controls because his legs were now useless. She went on to explain that he still drove around like a race car driver. She was bragging about it. She claimed he was a talented driver and could have been a pro if he had set his mind to it. In her eyes, I could see she adored her brother and thought he was just the greatest. Yes, he drove fast, she explained, but he was an excellent driver, a defensive driver, she said. I thought to myself, *how do you explain his crashing into a utility pole if he was such a great driver?* And now, with his newly customized muscle car, it didn't seem to bother her that, if he kept on driving like he always had, he might one day kill himself or someone else. I was disturbed by this whole conversation.

There was too much of that in the 70s. There were too many cowboys and there were too many people who idolized those cowboys. There was too much recklessness and little accountability. The many lives that were lost or ruined. It was not a heroic time. It was a sad and stupid time in my opinion. Oh, I'm sorry. Maybe I'm just an old man who is becoming cranky in his twilight years. But I don't feel like that about the present day. Things have changed.

So, why did things change? When did things change? In the 1980s, an organization called Mothers Against Drunk Driving (MADD) came into existence. It was started by a group of moms whose children had been victims of drunk drivers. It was a grass-roots movement that took hold both in the US and in Canada and it almost single-handedly changed the culture. MADD became such a vocal and influential group that politicians could no longer ignore their lobbying and it all trickled down to the courts. Then laws were rewritten. Fines were increased. Jail sentences were doled out. Drivers' permits were revoked. I wrote an article about it at the time. I titled it "Mothers Who Are Heroes."

Jacques and I talked about it often: the ridiculous number of fatal crashes that occurred every weekend on Quebec highways. And especially on long weekends. At one point, the SQ had orders to patrol with their flashers on, to signal their presence on the roads. That in itself didn't do much, but they felt they had to do something. Quebec had a horrendous reputation for fatal accidents and for reckless drivers. Jacques told me that on several occasions, as a patrol officer, he had been doing the speed limit with the flashers on and some idiot would have the gall to pass him. That's how blatant it was. Jacques always stopped the guy and gave him a ticket and a stern lecture, but still. Who would do that today? Pass a police car with its flashers on?

But slowly, things began to change. In 1976, the government introduced the first seatbelt law. Then Jacques told me that the Quebec government was about to take over the auto insurance business as it pertained to bodily injuries and death. He was right. That happened in 1978 with the inception of the RAAQ. The government now had a vested interest in bringing down the statistics of death due to car crashes. In 1982 a new Highway Safety Act came into existence which included stiffer penalties for all highway offenses including impaired driving. In 1990 the RAAQ morphed into the SAAQ and efforts intensified to try and stem the carnage on our roadways.

It was the era of wasted lives. That's what gets to me, I think. The Archie Wainwrights of this world. Not just what he did but what was done to him. Especially given what I learned from Finnian Toomey. I couldn't help wondering if maybe society had failed Archie Wainwright rather than the other way around. Instead of being thrown out of school, could he not have been treated by professionals? Would it have made a difference? I don't know. I would like to think that a child today who exhibited such dysfunctional behavior, violence toward his peers, would be referred to a psychologist or a therapist. From what Finn told me, I think it's clear that Archie was the one who was bullied: mocked and teased about his birthmark, regularly being called or referred to as a freak. Is it that hard to imagine that this might have had a devastating effect on a child? Turning him against everyone? I wonder how things would have turned out if Archie had had a softer, a more tender soul and, instead of rebelling, he had come home crying, time and time again, telling his parents that kids in school were always teasing him about his birthmark and laughing at him, calling him a freak. In today's schools, there are clear protocols about how students should deal with bullying. *Report them to a teacher or an adult*, they are told. But in Archie's day, there was no such protocol. *Fight your own battles*, was the unwritten rule. And so, he did.

The wasted lives: Remember Tony Curtis of Brome Centre? He was found in a back alley in Magog early one morning, laying in a pool of his own blood. He had been stabbed to death. I covered that incident at the time. Police said it was a drug deal gone wrong. I had no reason to doubt that conclusion. It was as though his whole life had been leading to that very ending. It was the kind of ending that I think Finn Toomey foresaw for himself, which caused him to change the trajectory of his life.

The wasted lives: In 1990, Alan Shearer of Sutton went to prison for 25 years. Police had brought Shearer in for questioning regarding a spate of B&Es in the area. The investigators told him that they had good reason to believe Alan was involved. In the days following his interrogation, someone told Alan that his friend and partner in crime, Timmy Benoit had probably ratted him out. Three days later, following an anonymous tip, the police found Timmy Benoit in a shallow grave on Old Notch Road, near the Scenic Highway, not far from Sutton. He had been bludgeoned to death with a ball peen hammer. They knew a ball peen hammer had been used because they found it right there, next to the body. The thing is, Timmy had not squealed on Alan Shearer. When the police questioned Alan about the murder and told him that Timmy had had his back all the time and had never betrayed him, Alan somehow found a modicum of humanity within himself, a vestige of human decency in his soul and immediately regretted having killed his friend. He confessed to the killing without hesitation. He was found guilty and served his full twenty-five for the murder. He never even applied for parole. He was released in 2015 and he moved back to Sutton where he lives a quiet life and works for a small construction outfit in town. No one in Sutton nowadays has ever heard of Timmy Benoit.

Wow, I'm trying to get to the end of this story but I keep digressing. Old men do that. I apologize. But at the risk of sounding redundant, I will repeat it: I am happier with the way things are now in Brome County. I have fond memories from the old days, yes, because of family and friends, especially my dear friend, Jacques Latendresse. I loved that guy. But it was a reckless time. And I was part of it. We were all part of it. Today, Brome County is a far safer and healthier place to live. I am fortunate enough to live here and to have known all these fine people. I was happy to be able to share this story and shed some light on some of the human beings who lived during that era, the ones who survived and the ones who, sadly, did not.

I have already asked the reader to forgive my numerous digressions peppered throughout this narrative. Now, I must beg indulgence for one last *transgression*: that I continue to refer to Brome County even though, technically, Brome County doesn't exist anymore. Who knows why they abolished Brome County? Governments never seem to want to leave well enough alone.

An old-timer in Austin, older even than myself, Roy Dudley, tried to explain it to me last summer. We were sitting at a picnic table on a sunny July afternoon, outside the general store in Austin, each enjoying an ice cream sandwich.

"Brome County got too big for its britches," he said. "We actually had the nerve to elect an Anglophone to the Quebec National

Assembly. That couldn't stand. His name was Glen Brown. Look it up."

I didn't have to look it up. I was around at the time, in the early 1970s. I knew Glendon Brown pretty well. I had interviewed him for the paper on three different occasions. I attended his funeral in 1981. But I knew better than to interrupt Roy while he was holding forth.

Roy continued. "So, they went about restructuring a new electoral district and called it Brome-Missisquoi."

"I remember that time," I said. "And some years later they removed Austin from Brome-Missisquoi and dumped us into the Orford electoral district. That pissed me off, I can tell you that."

"Of course, they did," said Roy. "Divide and conquer, that's what that's called." Roy rolled up the wrapping from his ice cream sandwich and threw it into the trash bin next to the picnic table.

He continued. "An Anglophone never had a chance in hell of being elected after that. We were now in the minority, outcasts in our own land. It was one step in the larger plan to strip the Anglos of any power we had and to eradicate the English language in Quebec. No Anglophones were ever elected again after they doctored those maps. It's called gerrymandering. Look it up."

I knew what gerrymandering was. I suggested to Roy that maybe Quebec would claim they were just trying to protect the French language. I really didn't buy into that theory but I felt I had to give

Roy some semblance of a debate, play the devil's advocate, so to speak. "After all," I said, "it is the language of love."

Roy replied. "Hell, French isn't the language of love. They don't even have a verb for love. Look it up. Whether it's their steak or it's their wife, they use the same verb *aimer*. That's it. "Plus," he added, "it is the English language in Quebec that is in danger of disappearing. Not the French. They got laws protecting the French language. Do we? No, we don't."

I don't know. Maybe Roy was right. Or maybe he was just old and bitter. Maybe both. Recently, I came across another passage from my favorite author, the late Cormac McCarthy. It's from *The Crossing*. I thought I'd share it:

The names of the cerros and the sierras and the deserts exist only on maps. We name them that we do not lose our way. Yet it was because the way was lost to us already that we have made those names. The world cannot be lost. We are the ones. And it is because these names and these coordinates are our own naming that they cannot save us. They cannot find for us the way again.

I was born in Brome County, and I will die here. I cherish this place with every fiber of my entire being.

Chapter 5
The Big Brome Fair

Sunday, September 1, 2024

Finn Toomey stood in front of the hallway mirror. Inspection time. Clean jeans: check. Clean boots: check. Clean black T-shirt with the MaxCo logo: check. No, wait. Second thoughts on the T-shirt. He turned and ran upstairs. He came back down to the mirror sporting a black cotton, long-sleeved shirt with button down collar and the MaxCo logo over his left pocket. There, that's better, he thought. True, it was going to be a hot and humid day but he had to look just right. He had to look his best. After all, today was the day he would tell her that he had been carrying a torch for her for such a long time.

What was the expression? Come hell or high water? Yeah, come hell or high water. Today, he would tell her what was in his heart. He wasn't sure how she would react. She would probably say thanks but no thanks. Hopefully she wouldn't outright laugh at him. That would be devastating. Hopefully, she would be polite and just let him down gently. It was not realistic to hope for anything more.

It had been six years since Jojo Alison had busted him for possession of cannabis, and since then, almost no day had gone by without him thinking about her. In July, he had seen her briefly at the Thirsty Boot, the night Stubs was killed. It was then that it hit him. That night. When he was leaving the bar holding Cassandra's hand which he promptly let go of as soon as he saw Jojo there. In fact, it had been like his hand had simply let go of its own accord when he caught sight of her, like he'd forgotten in that bright moment where he was or what in the world he was doing. That's when he admitted it: He was crazy about Jojo Alison. And Cassandra noticed it too when he let go of her hand. She called him on it. And Cassandra was also visibly disappointed when Finn drove her home and just dropped her at her door instead of going inside for a night cap as they had discussed. She just stood there with a puzzled look on her face as he drove away. But yeah, Finn knew for sure. It was Jojo. Nobody else.

Then, in early August, when he saw her at the funeral for Jacques Latendresse, again he was confronted with the reality and the depth of his feelings. That had sealed it for him. Even Alistair MacKenzie had remarked on some subtle bond between them. Finn knew he had to do something about it.

And now, here she was, at the Brome Fair, where he and she both were working all weekend. He'd seen her there on Friday but she was surrounded by other cops and he was too afraid to approach her. On Saturday, when he walked by the small SQ kiosk, she was talking with François Babouin. Again, he had not dared interrupt. But today was the day. He was going to speak to her. Come hell or high water.

He took one last glance in the mirror. The dude looking back at him flashed him a thumbs-up and murmured, "Go get her, cowboy. You got this."

He got into his pickup and drove west on Stagecoach Road. He turned in at the *Exhibitors and Vendors* entrance of the Big Brome Fair. Once again, Wendy was there to welcome him. With red-haired pigtails, in her mid-twenties, Wendy grabbed his side-view mirror and jumped up onto the side-step of his truck.

"Easy on the mirror there, girl," he said.

Looking around but not finding anything else to grab onto, she reached into the cab and latched onto the steering wheel.

"Hello there, handsome," she said, sticking her head into the cab. "Whoa, someone smells good in here."

"That's my air freshener," said Finn. "Eau de Canadian Tire." He then flashed his wristband at her.

"Not likely," she said, "and you don't have to show me that. I know who you are. Hey, where were you last night? I was expecting to see you at the barn dance."

"It was a long day, Wendy. I was beat. I went straight home."

"Well, I was really disappointed," she said. "Almost broken-hearted."

"I never said I'd come, Wendy. Plus, I've told you, my heart is taken."

"I'm not after your heart, silly."

Finn shot her a crooked glance.

"Your dancing feet, silly." she said. "No one can cut a rug like you, Finn. And I know your heart isn't taken, because I can see your place from mine. I see you all the time, all alone in that big house of yours."

"I didn't say I was taken, Wendy. I said my heart was taken."

"Well, heart or no heart," she said, "you better come dancing tonight anyway. It's your last chance."

A car behind Finn honked its horn. Finn looked in the mirror.

"Better get to it," he said, pointing with his thumb.

"Okay, but you better come tonight," she said, releasing the steering wheel and jumping back to the ground.

Finn waved half-heartedly and drove on. In the mirror, he saw Wendy shake an admonishing finger at him and then turn to deal with the next car in line.

Finn slowly drove to the MaxCo installation, right next to the main stage. He parked the truck and got out. There were four other outfits in the same area, all there to exhibit their farm and construction equipment but his boss, Max Couture had the biggest and finest collection of heavy equipment around and it was Finn's job to show it off. They were all painted in MaxCo's signature canary yellow and bore the MaxCo logo. The MaxCo exhibit boasted three different kinds of loaders, three excavators, a bulldozer, a feller-buncher, and Max's newest acquisition, a cherry picker that could rise up to over one hundred fifty feet. No other pickers in the region could match that. Good cherry pickers could reach fifty feet or maybe seventy-five but Max's could outperform them all.

Finn was making a cursory check of all his machines when his eyes fell on the corral that was set up behind the stage. There were two draft horses in the enclosure along with a familiar face. That familiar face saw him and waved so he wandered over to say hello.

"Truman Lightfoot," said Finn. "How are you on this fine day?"

"I'm doing great, Finn. Thanks. It's going to be a hot one. They're calling for as high as forty. We might even get a thunderstorm. Check it out." Truman pointed with his head. Finn turned and saw what Truman was referring to. Some big dark clouds heading up from the south.

"Whoa, yeah, that is some serious weather," said Finn.

"Hey, is Max coming out this weekend?" asked Truman.

"No, he's not. His granddaughter is getting married in Gatineau this weekend, so he left me in charge."

"Max still talking retirement?"

"He is that," said Finn, "and guess what? He's thinking he'll be ready in two years. And in two years I should be ready, financially that is, to take over the business."

"That's great," said Truman. "There's good money in heavy equipment, I hear."

"True enough," said Finn, "if you know what you're doing. And I think I do."

"I'll bet you do. It's all you've done for quite a while now."

Finn looked in the direction of the two horses. "So, who we got here today?"

"Finn, meet Jim and Jake. They're Clydesdales."

"Yeah, I gathered as much, just by their coloring. Are they sorrel?"

"Yeah, a little darker than sorrel. Technically, they're bay. They also have white blazes and four white stockings which is typical of Clydes."

"They new this year?"

"Yes sir," said Truman. "And I'm expecting great things from them. Possibly first place. They are bombproof. Know what that means?"

Finn nodded. "Of course. They don't startle easy."

"Exactly. As important a trait as any in a performance horse."

"An important trait even in humans."

Truman laughed. "Oh, you got that right."

For some reason, maybe because of Finn's mission to find and talk to Jojo today, he decided to get up close and personal with Truman. "Can I ask you something?" he asked. "Something personal?"

Truman turned from the horses and leaned down to a cooler at his feet. "Water?"

"Sure," said Finn.

Truman handed Finn a bottle of water. "Are we talking personal *me* or personal *you*?"

"Thanks," said Finn, uncapping and taking a gulp of his water. "Personal you."

"I'm an open book," Truman said, gesturing with open arms. "To you, anyway."

"We're about the same age," said Finn. "Do you have a partner? You know, someone you date? Go out with? Dinner? Movies? I've never seen anyone."

"I know what dating means, Finn, and the answer is no. I don't have someone like that. Truman took a slug of water and then continued. "You do know that I'm gay, right?"

"Yes, of course I know," said Finn. "You told me two years ago. Right here, at the Fair. We were in the beer tent as I recall."

Truman closed one eye as he tried to recall that conversation. "Okay . . . I must have had quite a few that day."

"You did," said Finn. "But still, there must be other gay men in Brome County?"

"Let me put it this way." said Truman. "It's slim pickings in Brome County as far as I can see."

Finn laughed. "I hear you."

"But once," said Truman, "I ventured a little further away to see what I could find."

"How far are we talking here?"

138

"Granby."

"Shit, Truman. Granby is not even an hour away."

"Yeah, well, it's a world away for Anglo boys like us from Brome County. Anyway, I heard about this club in Granby, a bar that catered to . . . my kind."

"Cool. And you went?"

"Oh, did I ever."

"Come on, how did it go? Did you meet anyone? What was it like?" Finn took another swig of water.

"Let me put it this way. The odds were good but the goods were odd."

Finn choked on his water, and spat it up, leaning forward so as to not slobber over his shirt. "Jesus, Truman. I don't know what that means and I don't think I want to know. But it's funny as hell."

"Yeah," said Truman. "I was wearing a nice shirt and a leather belt on my jeans and that was the only leather I was wearing. And as fate would have it, they were having some retro leather night. I felt so out of place."

"Oh, no. Did they give you a hard time?"

"Watch how you say that, Finn? A hard time is a good time in our language."

"Alright," said Finn, "So, did they give you any trouble?"

"Hell no! They treated me like the out-of-town guest that I was. They all wanted to buy me drinks. I spoke French to them and I told them I was from the other side of the Autoroute and some of them trotted out their broken English, just to be nice."

"So, no trouble then?" asked Finn.

"Trouble? Of course not. These were my people, Finn. Attire notwithstanding. I had never experienced anything like it. I had never been in a place where it was just . . . just us."

"Wow," said Finn.

"But I didn't find love or a life partner."

"Well, you're still young," said Finn. "Your time will come."

"Of course," said Truman. "But let me turn the tables here for a minute. Tell me about your love life. What's going on with you?"

"Well, in all honesty, I hope to be able to tell you later today."

"Really? Well, damn it, Finn, I wish you the best of luck." Truman gave him a playful punch to the side of his shoulder. "You deserve something good. Who is this person?"

"Actually," said Finn, "I'd prefer not to get into details because I don't want to jinx myself, but you'll be the first to know. Later today. Good or bad."

"Promise?"

"I do."

Finn saw two vehicles slowly arc around his machines and park behind the main stage building. One of the two vehicles was a van and was lettered, *Gemma & the Gemstones.* Finn pointed. "I know those people, Truman. Will you excuse me? I want to go over and say Hello."

"No problem," said Truman. "I'll catch you later."

You chicken-shit, thought Finn, as he walked over to see Wild Bill and the gang. *Come hell or high water, my foot.* He was supposed to be looking for Jojo Alison. But here he was, settling for any little thing to distract him from his mission.

"Hey, Finn," said Wild Bill as Finn approached. "Nice to see again."

"Hi folks," said Finn to the group. "Need any help unloading?"

"Absolutely," said Bill, "thanks so much." Wild Bill turned to his group.

"Hey guys, you remember Finn. Finn, you remember Augusto, Gemma, Lise and Isabelle.

They all said Hi to Finn.

Wild Bill continued. "Lise here is the drummer for the Gemstones. And now, she is also drummer for the Rebels. Isabelle is their bass player. You know Augusto. He's our bass player."

"Cool," said Finn although he was not sure he had ever met Isabelle before. "Nice to see you all again."

He smiled a little at seeing Gemma again. She wasn't dressed to perform yet. She was in jeans and a T-shirt. But her hair was ready. It was colored a bright green.

Finn had been wondering how Will Bill would deal with the absence of Stubs. He thought that maybe Steve Gibson from the Thirsty Boot would have taken over as drummer, just as he had that night at the Boot, but Lise must be a good drummer if Wild Bill hired her. "What time do you guys play?"

"Well," said Bill, "The Rebels go on at eight and the Gemstones at nine."

Finn was puzzled. "You guys sure showed up early for an evening gig."

Gemma explained. "We wanted to enjoy a bit of the Fair, plus we wanted to catch Abenaki, a First Nations troupe from Odanak. They will be performing some traditional music and dance at the Frizzle stage, around three o'clock."

"Oh, cool," said Finn. "Maybe I'll see you there. If I don't, I'll see you at your gig tonight."

"Great," said Wild Bill.

When they were done unloading the two cars and had stowed all the equipment in the storage space beneath the stage, Finn said goodbye to the five musicians.

"Thanks for all your help," said Wild Bill.

Finn waved. "My pleasure. See you all later."

As he walked back to his truck, Finn assured himself he was not avoiding his meeting with Jojo. He just wanted to wash his hands with his Fast Orange waterless hand cleaner he had in his truck. And then he would head over to the SQ kiosk, where he hoped to find Jojo.

But as he moved toward his exhibit, Finn couldn't help but notice the sky. The storm clouds he had seen a few minutes ago, were now rolling in towards Brome Village. By the time he reached his pickup, people all around were staring, mesmerized, at a sky which was greenish/black in color, like an old welt. He had never seen anything like it. It looked ominous. And then the day got dark. Almost as dark as it got during that solar eclipse back in April but faster.

Finn trotted to his truck and retrieved the key box that Max had left for him. He removed the key to the cherry picker. He rushed to it and powered it on. This model was battery-operated, and he saw that the charge was full. And he was also happy that he had set up the stabilizers when he had first arrived on Thursday afternoon. Safety first, he had thought at the time. He jumped into the basket and pushed the UP button. He climbed and climbed.

At about sixty feet he was high enough to have an unobstructed view of the surrounding area. This storm cloud was immense. Maybe a mile wide. It was coming from the south, and it was coming their way, no doubt about it. He estimated that the edge of this storm was halfway between Sutton Junction and Brome Village. Not far at all. It would be here, at the Fair, in minutes. Or less.

Then Finn saw something that made him shiver. In the distance, he saw two thin columns of cloud attempting to descend to earth but not actually making contact. He knew what they were. They were funnel clouds. He'd seen this on the Weather Channel. This was a tornado in the making. From up here, he had a full view of the fairgrounds and people were already reacting. They were scrambling for shelter. Wise move, he thought. He should do the same.

He brought the picker back down to its base and locked it in position. He removed the key and jumped to the ground. As he ran to his pickup, he saw the four other exhibitors now come rushing over in his direction. They must have seen him come down in the picker and wanted to know what he had seen. He stopped. He raised his hands high, motioning and signaling for them to stop. "Take cover," he screamed in English and French. "A tornado is coming. Take cover! TAKE COVER!"

Finn stood next to his pickup and watched as this dark sky rolled in. He figured he could stand safely here and when it got bad, he could duck underneath his truck. It was a four by four and had plenty of clearance.

His phone went off. It was a *Severe Weather Alert* from his weather app. No shit, he thought. Then he lost all connectivity. He tried to dial 9-1-1 but no luck.

Then the winds moved in. They blew and they turned and they churned and they roared and they howled like some invisible monster from above, about to unleash its wrath on all living things.

It started to rain and soon, the rain morphed into hail. Hail, hard and large, the size of golf balls. Smashing and pelting the metal of the equipment, his truck, the ground. It was time to take shelter. Crouching by his truck as it shook in the wind, he suspected it wasn't a safe enough place. He scanned the heavy machinery. The biggest, the heaviest, a Caterpillar dozer. A D-11. He ran for it, his back bombarded by hail as he ran. He dove to the ground. He clambered on all fours for refuge beneath the dozer. Hail still pelting down on everything. The storm continued to roar. What the hell was happening? This is Brome Village, not Oklahoma.

Still on his belly, he spun himself around to peek out from the rear of the dozer. He could see his truck. It was wet and pock-marked from the hail. It was heavy enough to resist being lifted but only barely. He could see it shaking in place. He was glad he decided to hide under the Cat.

And then, a monstrous crack. Then a creak followed by an immense thud. There. A giant elm fell onto his truck. Smashed and crushed his truck. For what felt like eternity he stared at the collapsed tires, the belly of the truck pressed into the grass that he himself might easily have been crushed in as well.

He felt safe, here under the dozer but how about the people? Families? Children? Had everyone found shelter? He worried for them. Where was Jojo Alison? Was she safe? Would he not see her again? Oh, no, this can't be how it ends? God, no. Not on this day. Monstrous winds, so loud he could barely think. From under the dozer he peered out again. Now, objects were flying in circles. Trash bins, baby strollers—oh shit—no! He shuddered at the thought of it. Sweaters, hats, paper plates, plastic cups, garbage of all sorts, flying, whirling about in the air. Now, more cracks, more creaks, more thuds. Trees coming down all over the fairgrounds. The sounds of the storm were deafening. It drowned out everything else in this world. The roar, the incessant roar, a wild beast of a storm, so insanely angry, lashing about, intent on total destruction.

It went on for minutes. Maybe three or four, he thought. Maybe five. Maybe one. It was so difficult to guess. The onslaught seemed eternal, never-ending. He had never experienced anything like this. But eventually, the evil beast, with its sounds and its ravenous appetite, its lethal intentions, seemed to recede. The storm and its sounds seemed to be slowly leaving, pushing to the north. The winds, slowly ebbing. The darkness, yielding to light. To sunshine once again.

Then he smelled it. At first he couldn't identify the odor that permeated the air but then he recognized it. It was the odor of sulfur. But that didn't make sense. Why would there be an odor of sulfur? Then he remembered something, again from the Weather Channel. The air was saturated with ozone. That was the smell.

And at long last a gentle calm slowly began to emerge and to replace the mayhem. And now, the sounds of the storm, the screams of the storm were replaced by those of animals, of families and children, their hearts having been struck by terror.

He slowly crawled backwards out from under the dozer. He looked to the sky. The storm clouds were gone and were moving to the northwest. The sky above the fairgrounds was clearing and the sun was coming out. The hail on the ground was melting. The winds were gone. The worst of it was over.

Now, again, he could hear people screaming from some of the other buildings closer to the entrance of the fair, near the midway.

He first checked on his fellow heavy equipment exhibitors. They were all fine. They too had hidden beneath the large machines they had brought to the fair. He talked briefly with them and they agreed that they would head to the center of the fair and see if they could help. Finn said he would go that way as well but he wanted to check the main stage first. He wanted to see if Wild Bill and his people were okay.

The sheets of metal roofing from the main stage were gone but the rest of the building seemed intact. He went to the rear of the building where just a short time earlier he had helped the Gemstones and the Rebels unload their equipment. He opened the door to the storage facility beneath the stage and saw that the equipment was there. He called out: "Wild Bill?"

"Over here," replied Bill, who emerged from around the outside of the building.

"You okay?" asked Finn.

"Yeah, You?"

"Yeah, I'm okay," said Finn.

"What the hell was that?" asked Bill.

"That, my friend, was a tornado," said Finn. "Where are the others? Are they okay?"

"They went to get some food and drinks. Before the storm hit. I don't know if they're okay."

"Well, let's go and look for them," said Finn. "We'll find them."

As they walked from around the main stage building, Finn noticed people were emerging from the grandstand and the numerous other buildings on site, where luckily they had found refuge. Most buildings were intact, although tin roofing sheets were missing from every one and the roof of the Arts and Crafts building was standing up like a half-opened tin can. Animals were in their barns and enclosures and Finn was relieved that their owners had succeeded in bringing them in before the storm hit.

Finn then looked in the direction of the midway. He could see some people huddled in groups, some children still crying even though the worst was over. Some adults were walking about in a daze, like zombies. He could see the Brome Fair security people were busy, moving about from group to group, helping people the best they could. Then, he heard a commotion coming from the center of the midway.

"Let's split up," said Finn. "I'm going to head over that way," Finn pointed to the Ferris Wheel. "See if they're there."

"Okay," said Wild Bill. "I'll check over near the food stands. I'll meet you over there after."

Finn turned and headed towards the Ferris Wheel.

The rides at the midway were still and silent. All around were clusters of people, families, tending to injured people. Nothing serious from the looks of it. Children were coming out of shock and were crying, distressed parents were trying to calm them. Trees were down everywhere. Finn could see more security people, in uniform, trying to help the various groups and families. Emergency people would soon be arriving. Fire Department, First Responders, ambulances, but there was no sign of them yet. He hoped they would arrive soon. Finn checked his phone. No service. He wondered if this storm had continued its destructive path northward or had it run out of steam. There was no way of knowing right now.

Finn was now able to pinpoint the source of the commotion he had heard. It was coming from the Ferris Wheel. He rushed in that direction. When he arrived at the large wheel, he could see that a large pine tree, an eastern white, had split and fallen into one of the middle spokes of the Ferris Wheel. Passengers from the lower baskets had managed to scramble to safety but the bulk of the passengers remained stranded and had apparently lived through the tornado, huddled in those baskets, high up in the air, shook by wind and battered by hail. The children were in a panic and were screaming. Parents were trying to calm them down. It was obvious that everyone on the Ferris Wheel wanted off but with the fallen tree in its spokes, they would have to wait to be rescued. They would need a fire truck, one with a ladder. But emergency vehicles were not here and Finn could not hear any sirens.

At the base of the Ferris Wheel, he saw that a small group had gathered and were all gazing up to the hub of the wheel. Then he saw it: a man was trying to make his way along the spokes to the people in the baskets. And among those watching was Jojo Alison. She was alone. Finn ran to her.

"Corporal Alison," he said.

She turned toward Finn. She had a panicked look on her face. "Finn," she said, "we have to stop him. There is hydraulic fluid all over the metal. It's not safe. He's going to fall."

"Who is that?" asked Finn.

"I don't know. The operator of the Ferris Wheel. He's trying to calm the people down. It's brave of him but it's dangerous. We have to stop him."

"Is help on the way?"

"No! I'm in contact with my detachment but the roads are all blocked by trees, cars and electrical wires. No one can get through."

"Are you okay?" he asked.

She looked at Finn. "Yes, I am. Are you?

Finn lifted his arms and turned in a circle. "All good." He was covered in dirt but he was alive.

Jojo continued. "Finn, we have to help these people. I think we're on our own. I sent my other guys on foot to try and clear the roads of traffic, so emergency vehicles can get through."

"We can do it." said Finn.

And then a voice from behind him. "Finn!"

Finn turned. It was Wild Bill, smiling and waving.

"Bill, did you find them?"

"Yes," said Bill as he approached. "They're all okay. They're helping others." Then he pointed to the man on the Ferris Wheel. "Holy crap! What's that guy doing?"

"Exactly," said Finn as he turned back to Jojo. "Corporal Alison, try and keep them calm. I have a *nacelle*. A cherry picker that can reach those people up there. I'm gonna go get it. I'll be back in five minutes okay?"

"Shit," said Jojo. "Don't go. I need you here. I'm afraid that man is going to fall."

Finn looked her in the eyes. "Corporal, I have to go get the cherry picker. I'll be right back. I promise. We can save him, and we can rescue the others up there."

"Okay," she said. "But hurry."

"I promise," he said.

"Wild Bill," said Finn. "Come with me."

Finn and Wild Bill found Truman Lightfoot at the barns where the draft horses were stabled. The roofs of those buildings had also withstood the onslaught except for some sheets of metal roofing having been ripped away, and the debris which now covered the roof. The horse handlers seemed focused now on calming and reassuring the horses.

"Truman," yelled Finn.

Truman turned. "Hey, Finn, you okay?"

"Yes, Truman. Hey, meet Wild Bill."

Wild Bill and Truman shook hands.

"We need your help, Truman," said Finn.

"What can I do?"

"Could you harness up Jim and Jake and meet me at my cherry picker?"

"Sure, but why?"

"A tree fell on my truck. We need your team to pull my cherry picker over to the midway. There are a bunch of people stuck . . . stranded on the Ferris Wheel."

"Holy shit. Yeah, we can do that," said Truman. He turned to Wild Bill. "You know anything about horses?"

"Not really. I'm a guitar player. But I'm a quick study."

"That'll do," said Truman, smiling. "Go wait at your picker, Finn. Leave Bill here . . . is it really Wild Bill?"

"That's what they call me."

"Are you really that wild?"

"As wild as they come," said Bill.

Truman laughed. "Leave Wild Bill here with me to help. Won't take but five minutes. We'll meet you there."

"Alright," said Finn. He turned and ran the path that led from the horse stables, past the rear of the center stage to the heavy equipment exhibit.

Finn still had the keys to the cherry picker in his pocket from earlier. He checked to ensure that it was in working condition and that nothing had been damaged during the storm. There was some hail damage: chips in the perfect paint, dings in the thinner metal and some cracks in the plastic housing near the control panel, but otherwise, it looked fine. He retracted the stabilizer arms and locked each in place. When he was done he heard a noise and turned to see Truman and Wild Bill, standing on a wooden sled pulled by Jim and Jake. The two Clydesdales seemed unaffected by the storm that had just passed. Bombproof indeed, thought Finn.

Truman halted the two drafts just in front of the cherry picker.

"You two," said Truman, "walk ahead and clear the way. I'll drive the team."

Finn watched as Truman attached a hook to the angle-iron, the place where normally a truck would hitch to the picker to pull it.

Wild Bill stood in front of the horses and held them calm.

"Have you ever done this before?" asked Finn. "You have any experience with horses?"

"Nope," said Bill, "Truman told me what to do. Just talk to them, keep them calm."

"Well, you're a natural," said Finn.

Then Truman yelled. "Okay! Let's move out. Slow."

Wild Bill walked just ahead of the horses as they pulled the heavy picker. Finn followed alongside, to ensure that all went well with the machine. Satisfied that the picker was rolling smoothly on its wheels, Finn moved up front to join Wild Bill.

Now Finn focused on the way ahead, to ensure there were no obstacles. They crossed the oval racetrack with no problem but Finn could see there were groups of people ahead. He went on and helped clear the way. Everyone seemed to understand and readily moved to the side. Security people from the Fair joined in to help clear a path for Finn and the team behind him. Finn signaled to Bill and Truman to keep coming.

When they arrived at the *Information* building and as they were about to turn left, Finn saw that he had made a grave mistake. There were obstacles barring their path to the Ferris Wheel. Damn, he thought. There were bleachers, benches and kiosks all over as well as fallen trees. They would never get through. Finn should have known better. They should have gone around the other way, by way of the stables.

Finn waved for Wild Bill and Truman to halt and then approached them.

"We can't go this way," said Finn. "It's blocked. We have to turn around. Go by way of the stables."

"That's not a problem," said Truman. "We'll turn right here. Wild Bill, can you walk point?

"That means walking up front, right?" asked Bill.

Truman nodded.

"You got it," said Wild Bill.

Finn was pleased to see Truman and Wild Bill working so well together. They had just met but they were now a highly functional team. No doubt about it, the two were getting along very well. Wait a minute, Finn thought. Wait a second. It just now occurred to Finn that he had never seen Wild Bill with a woman, like a girlfriend or whatever. Never. Was it possible? Is that why these two guys were getting along so well? He sort of hoped so. Both Truman and Wild Bill were fine people and they both deserved happiness. But no jumping to crazy conclusions, Finn thought.

They cut a tight circle to the right, making a U-turn, and headed back in the direction of the heavy equipment exhibit, back where they had started. Just after the exhibit, they turned right on the trail that led behind the main stage and came out on the road near the horse stables. As they moved, it occurred to Finn that they had been gone longer than the five minutes he had promised Jojo and he hoped she was doing okay. He felt a renewed sense of urgency. People on the Ferris Wheel were probably freaking out. They were relying on him. They turned right again and continued, Wild Bill in the lead, the horses following, Truman at the rear, walking with reins in hand and the cherry picker rolling smoothly behind.

At the Ferris Wheel they wheeled around while Finn found the ideal spot for the cherry picker. The people who were gathered on the ground cheered, seeming to know that somehow this piece of equipment was here to rescue the families stranded on the large wheel. Some people stranded up in the Wheel cheered also but he could hear children crying too.

"Whoa!" yelled Finn to Wild Bill and Truman. Bill stayed with the horses while Truman unhooked them from the picker.

"We'll head back," said Truman. "Get the horses unharnessed. Then we'll come back to help."

"Thanks," said Finn. "You guys were great"

Finn had just finished leveling the stabilizers when he heard his name. He turned. It was Jojo, running toward him. She threw her arms around him. His heart did a backflip in his chest.

"Thank God you're here," she said, squeezing him. "Well done."

"I'll be ready in a minute," said Finn. "I just have to put down this last stabilizer.

There was a scream from the people stranded on the Ferris Wheel as well as from the people who stood at the bottom of the Wheel. Finn and Jojo turned just in time to see the man, the operator of the Ferris Wheel, who had been traveling upwards, from basket to basket, was now hanging desperately by his hands from one of the large spokes. He had obviously slipped on the hydraulic fluid.

Then, as everyone watched, the man lost his grip and plummeted downward, and bounced off the guard rails below and fell onto the wet ground in a thud. Finn and Jojo ran to him. He was face-down and he was motionless. Finn knew he was a goner. He just knew. Jojo gently rolled him over and when Finn Finn saw the man's face, a man in his sixties, he noticed the birthmark, the big red blotch on the right side of his face, in the shape of an apple with its stem intact. Impossible, thought Finn. It couldn't be. Jojo checked for any sign of life. She checked for a pulse. She looked at Finn and shook her head. She then put her hand on his forehead and gently opened his left eyelid and checked for dilation of the pupil. Again, she looked at Finn and shook her head. Then he watched as Jojo looked around then ran towards the control panel of the Ferris Wheel. She grabbed something from the ground and came running back with a green hooded sweatshirt. She gently covered the man's face with the sweater. The sweatshirt read,

Brooklin Agricultural Fair

Brooklin, Ontario.

Both Finn and Jojo turned their heads to the calls coming from up in the Ferris Wheel. Some were shrill and panicky while others seemed calm and polite. Some just waved eagerly.

"Let's get to work before someone else falls," she said.

Finn took one final look at the man, rose and headed for the cherry picker. Jojo ran alongside him. Finn turned and asked. "Where are you going?"

"I'm going with you," she said. "Up there. It's a two-man job. I will keep them calm, you bring them down to safety."

"Okay," he said. Finn was not about to argue with her. Plus he was happy to be working closely with her. They both climbed into the basket of the picker. Finn pushed the UP button and maneuvered his way toward the top of the Ferris Wheel.

As they ascended he said, "Did you see the man who fell?"

"Yes," she said. "That was awful."

"I mean, do you know who he is?"

Jojo shook her head. "I have no idea."

"It's Archie Wainwright," he said.

"Who's that?"

"Long story," said Finn. "I'll tell you later."

"Okay," said Jojo. "Now get me close to each of those baskets so I can talk to the people and reassure them. And tell them to be patient just a little longer."

"Okay," said Finn.

"And we're going to start rescuing families with young children first," she said. "You okay with that?"

"Yes, Ma'am," he said with a weak salute.

Jojo smiled and playfully punched him in the arm.

And while Finn navigated the cherry picker around to all the stranded people, Jojo spoke to them and praised them all but mostly the children for being so brave. In English or in French, in whatever language they spoke, she told them that it would take no time at all to get them to safety. But not to be afraid and not to move. It would all be fine.

Now Jojo pointed to one of the topmost baskets. In it was a family of five including three young children.

"Let's do them first," she said, pointing.

"Alright," said Finn.

When they arrived at the top, Finn looked beyond the Ferris Wheel.

"Jojo," he said, pointing to the east. "There is a trail, a road, between the fairgrounds and Moffat Road in Knowlton. The ambulances, the fire trucks, they can all come through there."

"You're right," she said. "I'll tell them."

Jojo turned her head and spoke into her radio mic clipped onto her left epaulette. When the response came back it was garbled and barely comprehensible. Finn shook his head. He didn't understand. "Okay," she said. "They will try that way."

Finn and Jojo were now within a few feet of the family of five. Finn maneuvered the cherry picker to within inches. Jojo clambered out and jumped into the basket with the family. The children were crying but excited to see a police officer. Jojo knelt before them and held their hands. She reassured them that everything was going to be okay and told them how brave they were. Carefully, Jojo transferred the father, who was tall and could reach across the gap to hold the kids securely, then the kids went one by one, and finally the mother stepped into the cherry-picker with Finn.

"Take them down," said Jojo, settling herself onto the metal seat and holding the bar as the basket swung gently. "I'll wait for you here."

Finn slowly descended to the ground and helped the family disembark. Friends of the family were there to greet them. Both mother and father gave Finn a big hug. He pressed the UP button and went back up to rejoin Jojo. But Jojo was not in the basket where he had left her. She had climbed to the next basket and was now with a family of four.

"Please, don't do that," Finn said. "You saw what happened to the man. It's slippery out there."

"Okay, okay," she said smiling. "I won't."

Jojo began helping to transfer this family to the cherry picker.

"I heard back from the detachment," said Jojo. "About that trail. There are fallen trees blocking it. They are working on clearing the trail but it will take time."

"Okay," said Finn. "When we're done here, I'll go help clear the road. I have a feller-buncher."

"Great," said Jojo, smiling. "Whatever that is."

When the family of four was safely on the ground, Finn headed back up again to get Jojo and to get the next family.

They did this thirteen more times, rising to a basket, delicately transferring families or groups of friends from the Ferris Wheel to the cherry picker. Each time, Jojo waited up top for Finn to return.

As Finn slowly ascended, to meet up with Jojo for the final rescue, the phrase *every cloud has a silver lining* popped into his head. This day was definitely more than just a cloud. It was a full-blown disaster. But still, it had a silver lining. He had come upon Jojo unharmed and they both worked so well together to bring a large number of people to safety. She had smiled at him, had touched his hand and shoulder several times. She'd even hugged him, hard. Maybe he was reading more into it than he should but he thought he would have no trouble talking to her later, talking to her about his feelings for her and the possibility of a future between them. He still harbored no illusions about his prospects but he felt much more confident about his ability to talk to her when the time came. He was no longer nervous or afraid.

Now they arrived at the last group stranded on the Ferris Wheel. They were still quite high up, at the nine o'clock position on the Wheel. It was five teenagers: two boys, three girls, all in their late teens. They had all been patient and brave. Jojo helped the girls into the basket with Finn and then each boy. "There's no room for me," said Jojo. "Take them down and come back for me."

"You got it. I'll be right back," he said. "Wait for me here. Please don't move."

"I'll be right here. I'm not going anywhere." Jojo smiled at Finn, reached out and touched his hand. He reached for her hand and squeezed it gently. He smiled. He felt amazingly hopeful inside.

Suddenly the picker lurched and the girls shrieked.

"It's okay," Finn reassured them as he pressed the DOWN button. When they got closer to the ground the picker lurched one more time. They landed abruptly but they landed safely. As the five teens scrambled out of the picker basket, Finn glanced at the battery level indicator. It was low. The lowest of five bars. Maybe that was the problem, why the picker was acting up. Finn jumped out of the basket and went to the picker's main control box. He opened the cover and unrolled a fifty-foot length of electric cable.

Cable in hand, Finn ran to the massive generator that the Ferris Wheel was connected to and he plugged it in. He ran back to the picker and checked the control box. The battery level indicator was off and the AC light was on. Perfect. He now had power. He ran back to the basket, jumped in and pressed UP.

Halfway up to Jojo, the picker stopped and stuttered again. *Damn*, he thought. He had plenty of power. This didn't make sense. Something was wrong. Something had been damaged in the tornado. He removed his hands from the control panel and then again, slowly pressed UP. The picker ascended but it kept stuttering, kept jerking, lurching. But still, slowly he was approaching Jojo.

Jojo waved to him. "Stop fooling around and come and get me." She was laughing. But Finn wasn't laughing. He tried again to approach. The picker kept lurching forward and then back again. There was something seriously wrong with the machine.

Then they both heard the sounds. The sounds of sirens coming along the back trail from Knowlton. Many sirens. Help was on its way. Finally.

"Let's wait," said Finn. "This machine is acting up. A firetruck will be here any minute. They'll have a ladder truck. They'll get you down."

"No way," screamed Jojo. "I'm not getting rescued by some firefighter. Not when Finn Toomey is on the job. Come on, bring that baby a little closer." Jojo stepped out onto one of the metal supports and grabbed onto a rail above her head.

"No, Jojo," said Finn. "There is fluid all over the place. Don't do that. Please!"

"I'm okay," said Jojo. "We're so close. Just bring that thing a tiny bit closer."

Finn tried but it lurched and stuttered again. More than before. Now he was about five feet away from Jojo and maybe a foot below her. It was still too far, he thought. Too dangerous. He didn't trust this machine.

"The fire trucks are almost here," said Finn. "Please wait."

"No," said Jojo. "I'm going to jump to you. Hold it steady. We're gonna be okay. I can do this."

"No, don't!" screamed Finn. "Don't!"

With one hand holding onto the framework of the Ferris Wheel and the other in the air, pointing at Finn, Jojo got ready to jump. "Hold her steady, Finn," she said. "I'm coming to you."

"No!" said Finn but Jojo jumped anyway. She flew in the air toward the picker basket, both arms reaching out, ready to grab onto the top rail of the basket. Finn was waiting for her. She reached the basket and her hands clasped onto the top rail while her boots landed on the bottom rail. Finn threw his arms around her and held her tight. But then her boots slipped. She lost her grip. Finn lost his grip. She fell but her hands caught the bottom rail of the basket. Now her legs were dangling. Finn fell to his knees and then onto his stomach. His right arm shot out and reached though the picker's bottom rail and grabbed her gun belt. He had her. But he could no longer reach the control board.

"I got you," he said.

Inexplicably, the cherry picker started to descend. From his position he could see the master control panel down below, on the ground. Wild Bill was there, with Truman. Wild Bill was pushing the DOWN button. The picker started descending. Wild Bill gave Finn a thumbs-up. They were only about twenty feet off the ground. And with that Finn felt her weight increase as her grip on the rail began to fail. Then she lost her grip entirely. Nothing was holding her above the ground except Finn Toomey's right hand.

"Hang on, Jojo!" Finn screamed. Because he had latched onto the rear of her gun belt, her arms, her whole body was facing down to earth. But she was too heavy for one arm. Finn hooked his legs around the rails behind him and reached down and grabbed her gun belt with his second arm. It worked. He had her. With both arms. Now he pulled her up and with a swing, she reached out and got hold of the bottom rail again. He released her gun belt and reached for her arms, to help her climb into the basket.

Before she could pull herself completely into the basket, the cherry picker lurched twice in rapid succession and then a third time with the force of a whip. The power of it broke Jojo's grip with the picker. Finn reached out but in vain. She fell to the earth. He watched in horror as she fell, arms flailing, a look of terror on her face. Her legs hit first and then she flipped onto her back, her head hitting the ground as well.

Still on his belly Finn screamed to Wild Bill. "Get me down, Goddamnit!"

The picker lurched again, several times. When it was about eight feet from the ground, Finn rolled off the basket floor and dropped to the ground, feet first. He hit hard and he heard his teeth clack together but he was fine. Jojo was about six feet away and she was surrounded by people.

Finn did a panic-scramble on all fours screaming, "Get away from her." People moved and Finn crawled in closer. He could hear himself sobbing. But he was finally next to her. Her mouth was open and moving but no sounds came. She was not breathing. He put his hands on her face and whispered. "Jojo, I'm here. It will be okay. Breathe for me, Jojo. Breathe."

And then she gasped. She inhaled deeply. And then she breathed quickly for about thirty seconds and then her breath began to slowly return to normal.

Finn brushed her hair away from her face. "Talk to me, Jojo," he whispered.

"I'm okay," she said. "I got the air knocked out of me. I think I'm okay now."

"You scared me," he said.

"I know, me too," she said.

"Jojo, I'm sorry I dropped you."

"You didn't," she said weakly. "It was the machine. I could feel it." She shook her head. "Finn, I'm sorry I jumped. You told me not to. But I did. I was showing off."

"It's okay, Jojo, you're gonna be okay."

"I'm not so sure," she said and her eyes became moist. "It's my legs."

"No, you're going to be okay. I have plans for us."

"Plans?"

"Yes, I was going to talk to you about it this weekend. About you and me." He kept brushing away hair from her face although no hair was in her face. He just wanted to touch her face.

She tried to move. "Did you . . . did you really?"

"Yes, I did!"

"Oh, that is the sweetest thing."

"Yes, Jojo. I've changed. I'm totally legit now. I'm trying to be a good person, a good human being. I wanted to be worthy of you. I wanted to tell you that. I wanted to ask your permission to court you."

"Court me?" she said. "You sweet man. Yes, you may court me. But Finn, I don't think I'm going to be okay. I can't feel . . . Something is wrong."

"No, I won't allow it," he said. "I have plans for us."

"I think I'm paying now," she said.

Finn was puzzled. "What do you mean, you're paying?"

"This is my payment, I think. I have to pay for the boy, that boy we killed in Sutton. Oh, my God, Finn, I can't even remember his name. I'm so sorry. I'm so sorry we killed him."   Now Jojo was sobbing.

Finn became aware of the small crowd that had gathered around him and Jojo. They were uncomfortably close and Finn felt sure they could overhear Jojo's words.

"Move away!" he screamed, waving his arm. "Move away. Give her space!"

Then he saw Wild Bill and Truman helping to push people back.

"You didn't kill him, Jojo. You didn't do anything wrong."

"But I was there. Someone has to pay," she said. "I have a bad headache. Finn, I think I hit my head. I'm not feeling right."

"Ambulances are on their way. They're very close, Jojo. Help is almost here."

"Finn, what month are we?"

"It's . . . it's September. September first."

"My birthday," she said. "I think it's in November."

"I'll take you out for your birthday."

"Finn, I'm almost thirty-three and I never said *I love you* to a man."

"Oh, my God, Jojo. Then tell *me*. Tell me you love me."

"I love you, Finn."

"I love you too, Jojo." Now Finn was blubbering. "More that you can know. I loved you the first time I met you, that beautiful day when you arrested me."

They both struggled not to laugh at the absurdity of his statement.

"Me too, Finn. Me too." And then she gave him a smile, the same smile she had given him six years ago, out back behind the police station. The smile that had done him in, had totally disarmed him, rendered him powerless to resist.

From off to the right, he saw a uniformed First Responder come rushing in. Finn wiped his eyes and made room for her to examine Jojo. After a quick check of her vitals and a cursory examination of her leg injuries, the First Responder smiled at Jojo and placed a triage card, labeled IMMEDIATE, around her neck with a string. She then took Jojo's hand and said an ambulance was here for her. The First Responder waved at two paramedics who rushed in with a stretcher and carefully transferred Jojo to it. They then rolled Jojo to the ambulance, Finn walking alongside.

"I'm here, Jojo," he said, standing as close to her as he could.

As they were lifting Jojo into the ambulance, another team arrived with another stretcher, carrying Archie Wainwright. The green hoodie that Jojo had placed on him was rolled up and it lay on his chest. He too had a triage ticket strung around his neck. It read DECEASED. They lifted and placed Archie into the ambulance, next to Jojo.

The Paramedic driver of the ambulance apologized to Finn in French, telling him there was no room in the ambulance for him but that they were taking them to the BMP hospital in Cowansville. Finn nodded dully. His eyes were on Jojo.

The two paramedics shut the rear doors and got into the ambulance. Finn stood there feeling completely alone in the world and watched as the ambulance slowly exited the fairgrounds, lights flashing and siren wailing.

After a moment, Truman and Wild Bill came and stood next to him. Then came Gemma, Lise, Isabelle and Augusto. Finn turned to his friends. He said, "My truck is crushed. Can someone drive me to the hospital?"

"I can take you," said Truman. "I'll take you. Whenever you're ready."

Wild Bill spoke up. "Finn, we're going to leave you with Truman, if that's okay. We're going to check on some people we saw earlier."

"Yes," said Finn. "Thank you so much. You guys are great friends."

Finn saw Wild Bill look at Truman and say, "I'll give you a call later, okay?"

Truman smiled. "Yep."

Finn smiled inside. It looked as though Truman and Wild Bill had hit it off pretty well after all. He hoped so. For them.

Wild Bill, Gemma, Isabelle, Lise and Augusto gently patted Finn on the shoulder and walked off in the direction of the west side of the fairgrounds.

Truman turned to Finn. "Why don't you wait for me here. I just have to give the horses some hay and water. Then I'll get my truck and meet you right back here. Don't move."

"Okay," said Finn.

Finn stood there, and after a moment, he thought he heard the sounds of a drum. A big drum. A loud drum. A Native drum and rhythmic beats. His eyes followed his ears west, beyond the midway, over to the grassy area near the Frizzle stage, the smaller stage. It was Abenaki. The First Nations troupe. They had been scheduled to perform today and damnit, it looked like they were going to do just that. There were eight men in the middle of the grassy area at the foot of the stage. They were sitting around a huge drum all pounding in unison with drum beaters.

Then another eight members of the troupe emerged from behind the stage, adorned in feathered headdresses. They took their places behind the drummers and began singing an Aboriginal song. They sang loudly, almost screaming. It caught everyone's attention. Finn didn't understand the words they were singing but he allowed himself to imagine the words: *Mother Earth has sent us another hardship. We faced death but we are alive. We are the people who survive.*

Then, again from behind the stage, came a line of Abenaki dancers in full regalia. There had to be thirty of them: men, women and children. They danced in a line, in single file, around the drummers and singers, and then they moved out into the crowd that had gathered. Everyone applauded. From all around the fairgrounds, people left what they were doing and began to converge on the area, near the Frizzle stage, to witness this spectacle of Abenaki.

While the drummers drummed and the singers sang, the dancers–the women in jingle dresses–moved in a serpentine column. They weaved themselves through the crowd, who in return applauded excitedly. The dancers encouraged people to join them in the dance. And many did just that. Families with children, mostly. Those who chose not to join in, stood and clapped in time with the drummers. Finn saw Gemma, along with Lise and Isabelle, join the line of dancers.

What a spectacle it was! Spirits were high. Finn shook his head in amazement. It was unbelievable and it was a joy to behold. People from all over Brome County and beyond, came together with the Abenaki from their home in Odanak in central Quebec to what? Celebrate? Yes, to celebrate. It was hard to believe that a short time ago, maybe ninety minutes ago, everyone here was probably wondering if they would even survive the tornado. And now, as the sun shone brightly, they had all come together. Everyone joined in: all Fair volunteers, security people, First Responders. Everyone was there.

Truman arrived with his pickup, stopped and got out and stood next to Finn. "Holy crap," said Truman. "I mean, wow!"

"Yeah," said Finn. "It's a sight, isn't it?"

"Oh, yeah," said Truman. But after a minute, he nudged Finn. "Come on. Let's get you to the hospital."

They got into the truck and slowly drove out, and as Finn took one last glance at the fairgrounds, at the disabled Ferris Wheel and at the spectacle of Abenaki, it came to him like a flash of lightning. It was a moment of absolute clarity. He now understood what Jojo meant when she said she had to pay. Pay for the shooting. He got it. He understood. He didn't agree that she should be the one to pay, of all the cops who had been there. But that didn't matter. *She* felt she must. He, himself, was still paying for his time as a dope peddler. There was no getting around it: It was an awful business that he had gotten himself into, with no dignity in it at all. He profoundly regretted that period of his life. But maybe he also was being rewarded. Rewarded for his commitment to reform and to find an honorable and honest path in life.

He sat back and thought about Jojo, on that stretcher, as they levered her into the ambulance. He wasn't sure how she would emerge from her fall. He had to accept the possibility that she might be permanently paralyzed. But if that was her future, then it would be his future too. He would love her and take care of her. Forever. Even if she were in a wheelchair. He would chalk that up to his

172

reward for having tried to become a better man, for having tried to redeem himself.

And for just one brief moment, he relived the sight of Corporal Jojo Alison, as she launched herself airborne from the terrifying heights of the Ferris Wheel, her arms reaching out to him, to no one else, just to Finn Toomey of Brome Village, and he had caught her. He'd held her.

"So," said Truman, as they drove, "shall I take it that that lady police officer was the person you were referring to when we talked earlier today? You know, the one you didn't want to tell me about for fear of jinxing your mission?"

"Yeah," said Finn. "Her name is Jojo Alison. She's the one. She was the one all along."

"I'm happy for you, man," said Truman.

"And how about you?" said Finn. "Did you meet anyone interesting here at the fair? Any prospects?" Of course, Finn was referring to Wild Bill.

"Well, I think so but I don't want to jinx myself either so how about I tell you when I know for sure?"

"That sounds fair," said Finn.

Truman took his right hand off the steering wheel and pointed straight out the windshield. "I think I'll stay on Stagecoach Road," he said. "All the way to Gilman's Corner. Avoid the 215 and the 104 altogether. They are likely to still be a mess."

"Good thinking," said Finn. "Yeah, stick to Stagecoach Road."

Epilogue

In the Spring of 2025, in a quiet ceremony in Ottawa, the late Archibald Wainwright of Brooklin, Ontario, was posthumously awarded the Governor General's Medal of Bravery for his actions during the tornado at the 2024 Brome Fair, in Brome, Quebec. Present at the ceremony and accepting the honor for his late brother, was William Wainwright of Wolfvillle, Nova Scotia.

Also, at the same ceremony, recently promoted Sergeant Jojo Alison of the Sûreté du Québec, was awarded the Governor General's Medal of Bravery for her actions during the tornado at the 2024 Brome Fair, in Brome, Quebec. Present at the ceremony were a contingent of her fellow police officers from the Cowansville detachment, her parents Richard and Joanna Alison as well as her husband, Finnian Toomey who stood at her side for support as she had only recently graduated from wheelchair to forearm crutches. After she cautiously stepped forward to receive her medal, she reached for her husband's arm with her left hand. Then, with her right hand, she accepted the medal. She then broke decorum and protocol, when she turned and kissed her husband on the cheek. Everyone present applauded. Slightly embarrassed, Jojo Alison said to the crowd: "I'm sorry. We're newlyweds."

Acknowledgements

First and foremost to my editor, Gil Adamsom. Utmost thanks for all your help getting this work to where I hope it could be. You were always encouraging and a pleasure to work with. To Peter Stone, fellow writer and colleague from back in the day, when we both patrolled the roads of Brome County albeit under different blazons. To Alan Bowbrick, Chief of the Brome Lake First Responders; to Shawn Regan and Adam Enright; to Cindi Lewis, for your feedback and input. And to our local writing group, *Easy Writers* of the Town of Brome Lake who watched this story rise from the primordial ooze and eventually solidify into its current state. To Angela Leuck for her input on early drafts of this story. To Richard Hucal, friend for over fifty years, with whom I consulted on so many aspects of the story, technical and otherwise. To Cassidy Cadarette, Administrative Coordinator of Expo Brome Fair; Barrie Paige Past President of the Expo Brome Fair. To Dan Webster of the Thirsty Boot for permission to set critical scenes in his historic establishment. To my lovely daughter, Dr. Jen Gobby whose advice was always spot on and whose help with the cover design was much appreciated. And finally, Chief Daniel Gauthier-Nollet of the Abenaki Band Council in Odanak, Quebec and Vicky Défossés-Bégin, Director General of the Musée des Abenaki in Odanak, Quebec.

About the Author

Stephen Gobby was born, raised and educated in Montreal, Quebec. He has also lived in Alberta and in Arizona. He has worked as a teacher, police officer, insurance investigator, martial arts instructor, musician, and editor. He now lives in Knowlton, Quebec, close to his children, Chris and Jen, where he is currently working on *Missisquoi County*, Book 2 in the series Tales from the Townships. Stephen Gobby can be reached at

stephen.gobby@gmail.com.

www.ingramcontent.com/pod-product-compliance
Lightning Source LLC
Chambersburg PA
CBHW071354120626
46546CB00002B/685